FIXED

IN THE

TEMPEST

DIAMOND
KEY PRESS

Published November 2013

First Edition

ISBN-10: 0985625945
ISBN-13: 978-0-9856259-4-8

When I read Shakespeare's Sonnet 116, I immediately think of my husband of 26 years, Bret. He and I have weathered our share of storms throughout the course of our marriage. And he has truly shown me that love is an "ever-fixed mark." No matter what has come our way, he's always loved me and believed in me. He's proven what Paul wrote in Corinthians that love never fails. I am forever grateful that God brought him into my life.

Bret - I dedicate this book to you. You're still the one, and I love you.

Special thanks to everyone who makes these projects come to life – to Leonard for making sure the covers are spectacular, to Ashlee for defeating the epub monster and to Rachel for not wincing too bad for my lack of Oxford commas.

Thanks to my kids – Jessica, Jeremy and Allie – just because.

Thank you to my parents, Nona and Leonard Zimmerman, who've weathered the storms of life and have shown me what it's like to be fixed in the tempest. The cover photo is from their wedding, Jan. 25, 1964.

1

"Are you sure we have everything?" Lisa asked.

She stood surveying the neat stack of boxes in the back of the SUV.

"Mom, it's not like I'm moving to Africa or anything," said Brittany as she stuffed one more duffel bag into an open space in the vehicle. "Besides, we can always go shopping."

"There's so much we have to do. I don't know if we'll have time to shop. Your dad is going, and you know he isn't into shopping."

"Yeah. It's all good, Mom. Where's Dad anyway? We need to be going. Orientation is in four hours. I know it only takes two to get there, but I need to unpack and change. I'll have to do my hair again. I have to look great – first impressions, you know."

Brittany hopped into the passenger side and flipped open the mirror on the visor to check her light brown hair, which she'd spent hours straightening with a flat iron.

"I'll go see if I can find him," said Lisa. She realized Brittany wasn't paying any attention to her statement as she walked back into the house, where she found her husband, Tom, on his phone.

"I'm not sure. I have to take my daughter to college today. I will have to call you when I get back," she overheard him saying.

He turned to see her standing there. He looked startled.

"I've got to go," he said abruptly and hung up his phone.

"Is everything okay?" Lisa asked.

"Fine. Just the office. I told them I wouldn't be back today. Being the boss has its drawbacks, but you know that already."

"You are still coming with us, aren't you?"

"And miss sending my baby girl off to college?" Tom flashed that charismatic smile of his. "Never."

"She's ready to go. Now."

Tom laughed. Patience was not one of Brittany's virtues.

"Of course she is. I'm sure she's leaving a few things that she will blame on you for rushing her out the door. You know how much she likes to shop."

"Yes, and I know how much she likes to blame things on me too."

Tom gave Lisa a quick peck on her forehead as he walked toward the door. Brittany had always been Daddy's little girl. Lisa wished she had the same type of relationship with her daughter that Tom did. Brittany and Lisa seemed to fight more the older Brittany got. There was an uncomfortable gulf between the two of them most of the time. Lisa never seemed to know what to say to her; it always came out wrong. Tom, however, could do no wrong in his daughter's eyes. He was still her hero. Lisa was happy they had that relationship, but it was hard feeling like an outsider looking in.

As they began their two-hour drive, Lisa brushed a few tears from her eyes. This was it. Her youngest was going away to college. She would have an empty nest. Tom and Lisa's oldest son, Spencer, had graduated from college in the spring and moved across the country to take a job in an architectural firm.

Lisa had spent the past 22 years raising children. She'd worked as a reporter for a local newspaper until her babies were born; then she freelanced for the paper, but with the digital age came numerous cutbacks with the amount of work she was given there. She tried to branch out in other areas, but they were hiring younger people to do the work. She was already feeling a little useless and now Brittany would be gone. She wasn't sure what she was going to do with herself.

She felt a hand grab hers and looked up to see Tom smiling. He kissed her hand and winked at her. She took in a deep breath. It's going to be okay, she thought.

"Do you have the dorm information with you?" Lisa asked.

"Yes, I'm in Brant Hall; room 324. You've asked me this already. My roommate is some chick named Anne, and she's from Alabama. We emailed a couple of times. She's going to major in sociology. She wants to pledge to one of the sororities so she may end up in the sorority house and not be my roommate long at all," Brittany said in her usually annoyed voice.

After that brief exchange of words, Brittany spent most of the rest of the ride texting her friends. There were a few giggles here and there. Her best friend, Madison, was going to the same school. They weren't roommates, but they were excited when they found out they would be in the same dorm a few doors from each other. Lisa tried not to think about anything other than the moment. She'd spent the summer trying to avoid the thought of what the fall would hold. Once Spencer went away to college, he was gone; she knew it would be the same for the ever-independent Brittany.

Once they arrived on campus and found the dorm, Tom and Lisa helped Brittany transfer her life from home to college. There were parents and teens all over the campus. The teens were excited, but many of the moms wore a plastic veil of happiness designed to hide their inner tears. Lisa had put hers on as well.

Brittany saw Madison almost immediately after their arrival. From the shrill screams and exuberant hugs the two gave to each other, you would have thought it had been years or at least months since they'd seen each other, not the previous 24 hours.

"Did you see all of the cute guys?" Madison screamed.

"Yes! I have to change. They so cannot see me like this," said Brittany.

"Hey, what about me, the love of your life?" Tom asked.

"Aw, Dad," said the embarrassed teenager, who gave him a quick hug and kiss on the cheek before she ran off down the hall.

"I love you too, Brittany," Lisa said as she waved to the fleeting figure.

"Don't let it get you down," Tom said. "She did the same thing to you on the first day of kindergarten."

"True, she's never needed me."

"That's not true, and you know it. She's always needed you. She just doesn't show it the same way you do."

"Yes, she needs me when she wants me to do something for her or buy something for her."

Tom laughed at Lisa's comment.

"She acts the same way with me most of the time because she knows she can get it. She doesn't always get her way with you," said Tom.

Lisa and Tom brought the rest of the suitcases and boxes into the room. Lisa started to unpack them. She felt a hand on her shoulder.

"Why don't you let her do that? She will just move everything the way she wants it anyway," he softly suggested as he noticed the tears she was trying to brush aside. "She's going to be fine, and so are you."

Brittany had already registered for classes, and everything was in order for her. The school separated the parents and students into two separate orientations. Lisa and Tom had already read most of the pertinent information online, and Lisa didn't want to go to breakout sessions with patronizing titles such as "How Not to Be a Helicopter Parent."

"Let's go home. Our work is finished here," he said.

The two-hour ride home was quiet. Tom tried to smile at her several times, but other than that, he seemed distant.

"You didn't sleep again last night, did you?" she asked.

"No," he said. "I just can't get that girl's face out of my mind. I keep thinking it could have been our daughter. I can't get the image of her parents at the funeral out of my mind either. It tears me up inside."

Tom had witnessed a car accident a few months before. Courtney was a 17 year-old with a bright future. She was getting ready to graduate high school and had a full ride to college on a volleyball scholarship. She had just received the letter notifying her of her scholarship and was texting while driving to let her friends know the news. She swerved to miss Tom and hit a pole. She wasn't wearing a seatbelt and was speeding. The impact sent her into the windshield. Tom stopped his car in the middle of the road. He called 911 and stayed there until the paramedics arrived, but they came too late. She wasn't conscious when he reached her. Her door was locked and the window rolled up. He beat on the window and helplessly watched as she struggled to take one last breath. The image of her bloodied and mangled face and the cell phone flung onto the passenger seat, its face bloodied and shattered was something he couldn't erase from his memory. Seeing her parents at the funeral was even harder for him. They were devastated.

Lisa had felt Tom slipping away before he witnessed the accident, but he seemed even more out of reach now.

When the two of them arrived home, Tom headed straight to his office.

"Tom?" she questioned.

He stopped and turned with a puzzled look. She walked over to him and linked her arms around his neck.

"It's just the two of us now," she said and smiled. She gently kissed him.

"Remember the office called while we were leaving?" he said as he took her wrists into his hands and kissed the palms of her hands. "I have a proposal I have to finish by the morning. It's going to be a long night for me. Don't wait up."

"But you own the company," she protested.

"All the more reason why this has to be done right," he said and kissed her forehead. As he closed the door behind him, he smiled at her, but she felt as though he'd stabbed her in the heart.

Tom had his own real estate company. He brokered existing

properties, but in the past few years, he'd expanded to develop commercial projects as well as residential communities. At 47, he still had beautiful dark hair, piercing blue eyes and kept in great shape. He was a natural salesman. There was something about that disarming smile of his. Even when the housing industry suffered severe losses, Tom managed to keep ahead of the game. They had talked about retiring when he turned 50, but he seemed to throw himself even more into work the closer he got to it. They used to talk about traveling the world together, but somewhere during Brittany's high school days, the talks stopped. Lisa couldn't pinpoint the date. Brittany's senior year was a blur to Lisa. She had been so busy. There were Brittany's high school graduation and college visits and Spencer's college graduation. They had to help him as he transitioned from college into his life. It had been a brutal few months on Lisa's emotions. She wanted to be in his world, but he was preventing her.

Inside his office, Tom took out a bottle of Scotch from its hiding place. He'd turned to it more in the ensuing days after the accident. He told himself the alcohol helped him cope, but he was lying to himself.

True to his word, Tom worked until the wee hours of the morning and left for the office before she got up. It wasn't unusual for him; he'd done it for years. He'd grab a few hours of sleep there before heading into the office. But as in most recent nights, he couldn't sleep even the alcohol wasn't dulling his senses enough. When he did close his eyes, he not only saw Courtney as she died, but he saw other scenes he'd worked years to bury into the deep recesses of his mind.

2

"I'm sorry, Lisa. You know how much we value you and your work, but look around. We are operating on bare bones, bare budget and hardly getting out a newspaper, if you could even call it that anymore," said James Harrison, who'd been Lisa's editor at The Times for more than 25 years. "The newspaper itself is only a shadow of what it once was. It has fewer pages, and the page size has been reduced, but you know all of that."

James shook his head as he looked at the paper he held up for Lisa, and he sighed.

"I remember when we actually had space for copy," he said and placed it back on his desk.

Lisa looked out over the newsroom at the reporters' desks. Of the 30 cubicles, only six or seven had people seated at them. Empty cubicles once meant reporters were out gathering the news, but the desks they left behind showed signs of life. Stacks of newspapers, piles of reporter notepads, coffee mugs and lots of notes and messages tacked on the computer monitor meant someone was working there. Not so today. The cubicles were void of the human touch. They were stark desks with only a computer monitor and telephone at them. A few had an Associated Press stylebook and a Webster's dictionary.

She remembered her days on the job in the late 1980s and early 1990s before Spencer had arrived. Although it was a nonsmoking worksite now, then the newsroom was filled with a thick haze of cigarette smoke from the constant puffing of chain-smoking reporters and editors. Phones incessantly rang, and police scanners emitted a low hum and chatter about the pulse of the city. Sometimes, Harrison would bellow the last name of a reporter or two after he'd hear of a possible homicide on the scanner. He'd bark instructions and make sure they knew their deadline before shooing them out the door. He got louder after the stories were turned in. Reporters looked like whipped puppies with their tails tucked between their legs after Harrison finished quizzing them about the holes they'd left in their copy. They were often sent back to call their sources at late hours much to the annoyance of their sources, but there was a gap in the story that had to be filled.

The final flurry of tension came while copy editors finished off page details and sent clerks with paperwork to the back shop where people pasted stories and headlines the page. Copy editors often uttered expletives as the back shop called notifying them their headlines were too long, or that they need to take a look at the page because a story was too long and needed cuts – literally, as the story pasted to the mock-up page was too long, and a blade would have to be used to sever the words and drop them to the floor, often to the chagrin of the reporter.

Lisa had never heard anyone yell "Stop the presses." That scenario was fodder for movies, but she'd heard plenty of colorful phrases as an editor looked at a page proof and caught an error minutes before the page was set to print. But those days were long gone too as the nature of the newsroom had changed to its digitized space.

Even on semi-quiet days in Lisa's young career, there was electricity in the air because reporters were working on investigative pieces in an effort to trump the city's competing paper, The Gazette. It was a sad day when The Gazette finally folded.

On this day, there were only two writers churning out their copy as they blocked out the newsroom noise with their ear buds.

"Isn't there anything I can do?" she pleaded. "I was hoping to ask for a full-time job in the next few months."

"With budget cuts, the only way we are putting out local news is by overloading the few remaining staffers we have and killing the unpaid interns with stuff they can't even handle. I had one yesterday who couldn't even rewrite a press release. They've slashed the entire freelance budget, and we've had to freeze all open positions for the next six months, maybe longer. Even if someone leaves, those positions will be frozen as well; they immediately go dark," he said.

"I've heard. Do you know of anything else I could do?"

"The magazine division has had its share of setbacks lately. I'm hanging in here with hopes of retiring in the next few years, if it doesn't all collapse before then," he said. "I wish there was something I could do. I know you can write circles around these kids in your sleep. If I had a job I could offer you, I would."

"Thanks, James. At least you called me in and told me face to face. It's better than an email or text message," she said and shook his hand as she walked slowly out of the newsroom.

She recalled the countless stories she'd written as she glanced at her former cubicle. She'd traded her cubicle in for a spot in Tom's home office years earlier, but that tiny desk still had a special place in her heart. She wrote her first front page story in that spot. She'd been following the saga of a 9 year-old who was awaiting a heart transplant. Casey had been born with a heart defect and had numerous surgeries in her young life including her first when she was less than a day old. The front page story was about her plight and her family's efforts raise money for a transplant. Casey finally got the heart transplant, and about two years later, Lisa and Casey made the front page again as Lisa wrote Casey's obituary. Casey had succumbed to an underlying infection, which weakened her heart. In the end, it was pneumonia that took the little girl who'd fought so hard. Lisa fought through her own tears to write the obituary. The family had become close friends of hers during their struggles and victories.

Lisa knew how to write stories that tugged on the heartstrings. There were so many over the years, but every time Lisa thought of Casey and her family, Lisa couldn't help but tear up.

Before she reached the door, another colleague stopped her. Jessie Rose had covered arts and entertainment for years.

"Hey, Lisa. I heard about the cuts," she said.

"Yeah. I don't know what I'm going to do with myself."

"Don't let those writing skills go to waste. You should write a book," said Jessie.

"Write a book?" Lisa shook her head. "No. I don't have the attention span for a complete volume. That would require such a time commitment."

"It's really pretty easy to do. I've written several," she said.

"I know, but you had a built-in publisher and marketing company because the newspaper does everything for yours."

Jessie laughed.

"True. Taking the interviews you've done over the years to create the books the publisher wants makes it a little easier."

"I don't even know where I'd begin."

"I hate to see you go. We've been friends for so long. I've always enjoyed reading your copy."

Jessie's eyes darted around the newsroom as though she was looking for someone. She lowered her voice to almost a whisper.

"What happened to the great journalism grads we used to get? They just don't make them like they used to," Jessie said.

Lisa tried to smile. Jessie and Lisa went to college together and took many of the same journalism classes together. Jessie was Lisa's editor at the college newspaper. They had a friendship that had weathered the years.

"I know what you mean. They just went downhill after us," she said trying to be cheerful.

Jessie gave Lisa a hug.

"If I hear of anything, I'll give you a call," Jessie said. "And Lisa, I've always considered you a friend so if there's anything else I can do, call me. You've always bounced back from bad times. I know you will this time."

"Thank you, I will. Take care of yourself."

Lisa nodded. She was in a haze during the walk from the news building to her car. She barely remembered the drive home. Her mind was consumed with an overwhelming feeling of worthlessness. Her children were gone; her job was gone. She had plenty of time to write a book, but she didn't have a clue as to where to start. What would she even write about?

She stopped by the store on the way home. Well, she still had Tom; the only constant in her life for the past 27 years. She walked up and down the aisles trying to figure out the perfect meal. She was determined to make a memorable evening with her husband. What did she have time to make? She didn't have enough time for a gourmet meal, but she could put a roast in the oven. Of course, they needed cheesecake for dessert. It would be perfect, she thought. He always liked down-home cooking. She didn't do it often, but she knew he'd enjoy it. She needed to reconnect with him somehow.

As she was planning it in her head, her phone rang. It was Tom. She smiled as she answered.

"Hey, I was just thinking about you," she said.

"I love to hear that," he said.

"It's been a bad day. I knew budget cuts were coming, and they completely did away with the freelance budget."

"Don't you worry about a thing," he said. "I'm working on a proposal that will make it so you never have to work again."

He sounded like the old Tom. Maybe, she'd just been imagining things.

"Well, I don't have to now, but I enjoy what I do. I feel like I'm being productive and making a difference."

"I know that you do, and you've always done a great job. We'll figure it out together. I'll be home as soon as I can," he said.

As she hung up the phone, she felt a weight lift off her shoulders. Everything would be fine.

She decorated the table with her finest china, candles and linen tablecloth and tried to find the most beautiful, sexiest red dress she could in her closet. She took extra care to sweep her chestnut brown curls into a soft loose twist. She wore some of her favorite pieces of jewelry that he'd given her over the years. She was getting the finishing touches ready when he arrived home. As he walked into the kitchen, she turned toward him. He was carrying a huge bouquet of red roses, which he placed on the counter. He looked surprised for a moment.

"What's the special occasion?" he asked as he approached her. His gaze seemed to caress her before he could touch her.

"Any night when I'm with you is a special occasion," she replied with a smile.

Tom paused and devoured every inch of her with his gaze.

"You look stunning." He touched her cheek and kissed her with a passion she hadn't felt in such a long time. He grasped her around the waist and pulled her close to kiss her for a few minutes.

Lisa closed her eyes and shut out all of her negative feelings – the worthlessness, fear and doubt. The person who mattered most to her was giving her his undivided attention – no work, no proposals, no shutting the door to his office. What they meant to each other was all that mattered then.

He picked her up and carried her to their bedroom.

"What about dinner?" she asked.

"It can wait."

The next morning, Lisa awoke to feathery kisses on her eyelids and a gentle brush of a hand against her cheek.

"Good morning, Angel," Tom said.

"Good morning."

He hadn't called her "angel" in months. Lisa blinked. He was dressed in a suit and neck tie.

"It's Saturday. Why are you dressed?" she asked. "You should stay here with me."

"Remember what I started to tell you yesterday?" he sounded excited. "I have a huge project that looks like will fall into my lap. Then, we can move away to that island we always talked about. It's going to be crazy, and I will be gone a lot. I may have to travel, but it will be worth it. I just know it."

He kissed her on the cheek and headed for the door.

Lisa tried to smile as the familiar doubt and fear returned like a knife in her heart.

3

"What is wrong with you, Lisa?"

Lisa usually met with her friend, Kathy, once a week for a date over coffee. Hiding anything from Kathy was impossible. Lisa had gotten out of their dates for a few weeks. On one of those days, Brittany was sick, and Lisa drove four hours roundtrip to take her to the doctor. And another, Lisa had her own dentist appointment, which she'd conveniently rescheduled to get out of their usual date without tons of questions, but she couldn't go for three weeks in a row without Kathy being suspicious. Kathy had already called and texted several times. Lisa just couldn't focus on their conversations.

"Nothing," she said and offered a weak smile.

"You never say 'nothing' to your girlfriend. I know when you are lying," Kathy answered politely.

"I don't want to talk about it."

Kathy smiled and didn't say anything. The silence was awkward, and Lisa's emotions had been brewing over the past few weeks. She hadn't had anyone to confide in so Lisa began to pour out her feelings.

"I just feel overwhelmed, useless. It's everything. Brittany going off to school and Spencer moving across the country. Why do empty nest and emptiness sound so much alike?" Lisa asked. "I haven't heard from Spencer in several weeks, and the only time I hear from Brittany is random text asking for money."

"That sounds typical."

"And I used to find so much meaning writing for the paper. I felt like I was doing some good for the community by writing the good news. You know me. I've always written the uplifting stories about people who overcome the odds or charities making a difference. Now that I don't have that, I feel utterly useless."

"I understand that in a way. I thought you were going to start doing some charity work of your own," said Kathy. "And didn't you have a job interview for a public relations position at the hospital?"

"I did. I never heard anything else, and as for charity, the only non-profits I've been in are arts-related. They have too many memories associated with the kids and the paper. I'd be thinking about what was missing from my life again."

"Somehow, I don't think that's all that is bothering you," said Kathy. "Seems like there's an 'and' or a "but" in there too."

That's what Lisa didn't want to talk about.

"I said I didn't want to talk about it," Lisa's tone was sharp.

"You haven't wanted to talk about it for weeks now. I know all of the other stuff going on," said Kathy in almost a whisper. She reached her hand across the table and placed it on Lisa's hand. "I'm here to help you."

Tears tumbled from the corners of Lisa's eyes and coursed down her cheeks. She'd been holding it in, and once the tears started, there wasn't much she could do about them.

"No one can help me," she said. "But it's Tom."

Kathy nodded. She knew because Lisa had been avoiding talking about Tom since Brittany went to college.

"I can't force you, but I know you need to confide in someone."

"I know. It's just that I have no proof of anything. Nothing unusual is happening. He's always worked a lot. He's always spent nights in his office downstairs. But I just have this ache in the pit of my stomach. Something isn't right. I have nothing to go on except this gnawing," she said as she grabbed some of the tissues Kathy offered her. "He's shutting me out."

"Have you ever felt like this before?"

"No. It's never bothered me. I've never thought anything was wrong. He's always been honest and upfront. I've never caught him in a lie."

"Do you think there is someone else?"

"I don't know. Yes, well maybe. I don't know. I've never ever thought anything like this in my life. He's always been so good to me. We've always been so good together."

"Nothing has happened differently?"

"He's just pulled back. I know he's been dealing with that accident he witnessed. It's caused an emotional cloud. I'm so confused. Maybe it's everything coming together at one time. Maybe things aren't really different. I'm only noticing the slightest thing now. Like I said, I can't put my finger on it. I do know the affection we've felt for each other hasn't been there are much. When he comes home from work, it's straight into the office. We've only slept in the same bed once since Brittany went to school two months ago in early August."

Kathy nodded.

"I don't want to lose Tom," Lisa said.

"I know, honey."

"He's the only man I've ever loved. I don't know what I'd do without him," Lisa continued to cry.

Kathy didn't know what to say. Her words seemed empty. She silently said a prayer as she listened to her friend pour out her heart.

"I'm sorry. I need to leave. I need to sort things out on my own," Lisa said as she picked up her purse.

"Are you sure you are okay to drive?" Kathy asked.

Lisa nodded and gave her friend a hug.

"Thank you."

It was close to 11:30 a.m. so she decided to go to Tom's office in hopes of having an impromptu lunch date. She touched up her makeup in the car before heading in. Her eyes were still puffy from all the tears.

"Mrs. Kinsey, it's great to see you," said Tom's assistant, Rebecca, as Lisa entered the office.

"Is Tom here?"

"Yes, he's in the conference room."

"Thanks."

The conference room door was open, and Lisa peered in to see Tom looking over some blueprints with an attractive woman. She was in her late 20s with shoulder length blonde hair. She was wearing a tailored suit with her blouse open a little too low for Lisa's liking especially when she saw how close they stood to one another. They seemed to be almost touching. She was laughing when Lisa cleared her throat.

"Hi, honey," said Lisa as she marched into the room.

Tom stood up. Was it her imagination or did Tom look a little uncomfortable to see her? She thought she saw a look of panic in his eyes, but it dissipated as he flashed that smile of his. There was something about his smile. She hadn't seen it in a while. He walked over to her and gave her a kiss, albeit a brief one.

"Lisa, I want you to meet Christine Pennington," he said. "She's the liaison between the company's London office and here."

Lisa forced herself to give her best reporter fake smile as the uncomfortable feeling in the pit of her stomach grew worse.

"It's nice to meet you," Lisa said as she reached out her hand to shake Christine's.

"So lovely to finally meet you. I've heard so much about you," Christine answered and returned a limp and lifeless handshake, which she obviously wanted to end before it began.

Lisa wondered what Christine had heard about her as turned her attention back to her husband.

"I was wondering if you were doing anything for lunch? I was out anyway. I thought I'd surprise you, and it appears I did."

Tom didn't respond to her sarcastic ending phrase.

"We have a lunch meeting. That's the reason we are going over these plans once again," said Tom. "We've got a few adjustments before any contracts can be signed."

He moved back toward the conference table and pointed at the stack of papers on it.

"Oh I see."

"And Lisa, I may be working late again tonight," he added without looking at her when he spoke.

Lisa glanced at Christine. She thought she saw a quick smile which faded when Christine realized Lisa's piercing glare.

"Okay. I'll see you when you get home then."

"Don't worry about waiting up. It could be a long night," he said.

Lisa felt the color drain from her face as she nodded and quickly left the room. She didn't think he even noticed her before they returned to their plans. She rushed past Rebecca on the way out and didn't even acknowledge her as Rebecca said goodbye.

Lisa was sure her greatest fears had been realized. She knew Tom was having or would be having an affair with that woman in his office. She felt angry and helpless and a whole array of emotions she couldn't describe.

The next few hours were hazy for Lisa. She turned off her cell phone after she noticed Kathy had tried to call her twice. She didn't want to talk to anyone. She got into her car and drove until she found herself parked at the lake near one of the recreation areas. How she got there she couldn't remember. She sat in the vehicle for several minutes. She wasn't sure how long. Time had no meaning. She had no place to be, no deadlines to meet. She saw a picnic table and decided to get out of the car. In October, there was no one else there. It was a typical Georgia fall day. The temperature was in the 70s, and it was slightly overcast, which seemed appropriate considering her mood. As she sat at the table, the tears began to roll down her cheeks. She didn't know what to do or where to turn. She thought about her life to this point. If someone had asked her at 16 where she'd be at 46, this is not the picture she would have imagined as she heard the final fragile pieces of her life crashing to the floor. Without Tom, what did she have now?

She grew up in the church. She had so many plans when she was younger. This was not the road she thought she'd go down. She went on her first mission trip when she was 16. It was to Honduras. There, she helped feed children in orphanages, but more than that, she prayed and watched the amazing things God did for them. Many were sick and malnourished. She thought about how she took the babies and sang to them as she rocked them. They were so hungry, but not just for food. They were hungry for a human touch and for a supernatural touch. She wanted to bring them all home. She went on two additional trips the following summer. She also visited Mexico and Guatemala. She saw the same thing in those places.

She had planned to go to school to become a missionary. She went away for her first year, but her father was diagnosed with an aggressive form of cancer a few days after she left. It was crazy to her. He seemed perfectly healthy when she left, but he died only a few months after doctors found it. She returned home before the end of the first semester because her mother was devastated, and so was she. She took a few classes at the local college while she helped support her mother. She met Jessie Rose seemingly by chance one day, but it changed her life. Jessie was in the journalism program and was working on a story about cancer and how it impacts families for a journalism project. They were in line in the student cafeteria when Jessie started chatting. Her project deadline was looming, and they spent a couple of hours talking about Lisa's experiences. Jessie got an A on the paper, and because it featured fellow student, it ended up on the front page of the college newspaper.

It struck a chord in Lisa so she decided to major in journalism in hopes of helping people. She wrote for the school newspaper and loved it. Meeting Tom was another seemingly random encounter. He was a business major and a member of several business-related clubs on campus. One of the clubs held a holiday food drive, and he was the project chairman for it. The first time she saw his smile and blue eyes she went weak in the knees. It was embarrassing. She forgot the questions she wanted to ask him, and at one point, she dropped her notebook. It was like a scene from a bad movie as they both knelt down to pick it up at the same time and their heads collided. She was horrified, but he laughed the most beautiful laugh she'd ever heard. Somehow, she managed to write the story, and the food drive was a big success. He tracked her down at the newspaper office after the drive with a bouquet of flowers and bottle of aspirin wrapped in a bow. When she saw the aspirin, she laughed. He asked her out, and they were inseparable from that moment on.

She always felt insecure when it came to him. He was extremely handsome, and although he told her daily how beautiful he thought she was, she had trouble believing it. She never saw in the mirror what others saw. She thought she was fat. She wasn't a model, but she wasn't overweight. She had dark chestnut curly hair and green eyes that always showed compassion in them. Even at 46, she had very few wrinkles, and she looked much younger than her age. She inherited fair skin from her mother so she never tanned when she was younger. She avoided the sun for most of the time. Maybe that had helped in her efforts to fight the signs of aging.

As she sat blankly staring at the water, she wondered what would have happened if she'd followed the original plan. How would things have turned out? She never would have met Tom. She'd thought about the missionary thing over the years. Every time there was a plea on television for one of those organizations raising money to feed starving children in Africa, the pull to go back was in her heart. Now that her kids were gone and she had no job, the thoughts of the mission field kept pushing their way into her brain. It was strange because it had been so long since she really even prayed. Surely God had forgotten the promise she'd made to spend her adult years in the mission field? The family went to church together at times, but it had been more out of a civic duty than out of a love for God. It was empty, but everything else in her life seemed empty now. If Tom was cheating on her, what would she do? No job, no money, no children. He could take everything and leave her with nothing. She felt a chill as a wave of fear passed over her.

"Oh God. I don't even know how to pray anymore," Lisa started to say as she placed her hands over her face.

All she kept thinking was "empty," and now, she was uttering empty words.

She broke down and placed her head on the picnic table.

"It's not the end," she heard a voice say.

Lisa sat up. She was startled and confused. After all, it was in the middle of a weekday afternoon in October at the lake, and no one was supposed to be around. She looked up to see the weathered, but kind face of an older man staring at her. He was wearing a plaid shirt and jeans with a khaki vest and hat with fishing hooks in it. He was wearing rubber boots with his pants' legs tucked in them, and he was carrying a tackle box and rod and reel.

"I didn't mean to scare you," he said. "God hears even the smallest of cries."

Lisa wiped the tears away from her eyes hurriedly. She was embarrassed he'd come up on her like that. She looked into his face. He smiled, and there was a twinkle in his eyes.

"It may not look like it, but this is going to work out," he said and gently touched her hand.

"How do you know?" she whispered the question.

"I have it on good authority, and you are going to be just fine. Things will work out. Don't give up and don't lose heart," he said and walked toward the lake. "God has been waiting for you for a long time."

Lisa looked in her purse to find some tissues. When she looked up, she didn't see the man any longer. She looked along the edge of the lake and scanned a vast area. There were no other cars near hers in the parking area. Where did he come from? Where did he go?

She stared the glassy, calm lake realizing she felt that way inside now. That gnawing ache was gone. She had no fear, no dread, no emptiness. She took a deep breath. It was going to be okay, but how long would it take to get from where she was to that place?

4

Over the next several days, Lisa tried to figure out how to confront Tom. He was home so little, and she didn't want to cause a scene at his office. She ignored phone calls and texts from Kathy. Since Kathy's husband, Gene, worked with Tom, Lisa wanted to keep certain things to herself. She didn't want to be the fodder for everyone's gossip, not that she really thought Kathy would tell anyone. Kathy had never shared anything Lisa had told her in confidence, but in Lisa's profession, she learned many secrets never stayed secret.

Lisa needed to find a job or something to keep her mind off of her troubles. To maintain the peacefulness she discovered on the day at the lake, she found herself praying more than she used to. She started thinking about other people and praying for them as well. She also thought a lot about missions work. It started to take over her mind. She wondered how she could go to the mission field.

She'd gone out to run a few errands and was surprised to find Tom's car in the garage when she arrived home. She checked her watch. It wasn't even 4 p.m. What was he doing home?

As she hurried into the house, she felt her calmness leave. She threw her grocery bags onto the island in the kitchen and began to search for him. She found him in the living room. He was seated in one of the chairs. He looked awful. His tie was loosened, and his sleeves rolled up. He was blankly staring at one of the walls and seemed oblivious to her entry.

"Tom," she said softly.

He turned to her. Had he been crying? She wracked her brain. Had she ever seen him cry? He cried when his mother died and at the births of Brittany and Spencer. He cried a few tears when their Cocker Spaniel, Eddie, died, but she couldn't recall too many other times when she'd seen him cry.

He stood up, and she walked quickly toward him.

"What's wrong?" she asked.

She was right. He had been crying. He reached out and pulled her close to him. He buried his face into her thick hair as he held onto her tightly as though this would be the last time he'd see her. As he held her, she could smell stale alcohol. She felt numb. She knew she was right.

"I'm sorry. I'm so, so sorry," he murmured.

"What are you talking about?"

Tom released her and stepped back.

"I never meant for any of this to happen. It just happened. It wasn't planned."

"What?"

He paused. He seemed to be searching for words.

"Lisa, I have always loved you," he said.

"Tom, you are scaring me."

"This was all so sudden. So crazy."

"You are having an affair," she said with no emotion.

Tom looked at her in disbelief.

"How did you" he started, but Lisa cut him off.

"I've known for a while. I didn't have proof, but deep inside, I knew," she said in a hoarse whisper.

"How could you know?" he asked. "She's gone. Is that why you sent me that text?"

"What text?" she questioned. "I didn't send you a text, but I did sleep in your office last night. You never came home."

"I'm sorry," he repeated several times.

"Christine?"

"Yes, but she returned home today. I never plan to see her again."

Tom sat down on the edge of one of the chairs and stared at the floor. He rubbed his face and ran his hand through his hair.

"I'm just like my father," he said.

He looked up at her. Lisa stood motionless, trying to process all the emotions. She had known, but the reality hurt more than she could have imagined.

"I never wanted to be like my father. I never did this before. He would come home drunk. There were other women. My mother cried so much. He hurt her so much."

His voice trailed off as he glanced toward a wall.

"People have called me 'charming' and other words that made me replace them with 'cheater.' I know they think that about me. Men have said it in their nudges and winks or in disdain as they judged me. I hated what my father did to my mother. He hurt her so. I hate him now, and I'm just like him. That accident - seeing Courtney dead and feeling so helpless - made me remember the nights I cried in my bed because I could hear him beating my mother, and I couldn't do anything. I tried so hard to bury those thoughts. I blocked them because of the pain they caused. I tried to erase them, but they are still there."

He stood up and walked over to the fireplace. He balled one of his hands into a fist and slammed it onto the mantle.

Lisa walked up behind him and placed her hand on his shoulder.

"We can work through this," she said. Her voice sounded hollow.

He spun around and looked at her.

"Lisa, I don't know who I am anymore. The one thing I vowed I'd never do I've done. I can't undo it."

"What are you saying?"

"I need to find out what's wrong with me. I need answers, and I don't want to hurt you in the process," his voice was anguished.

"I'm confused."

"I am too. Lisa, I need to be alone for a little while so I can sort out what's going on with me."

"I'm your wife. I made you a promise. Remember – for better for worse? I promised to be there, and I want to help you."

She could see the mix of fear and anger in his eyes. She'd never seen that expression on his face in their entire 25-year marriage.

"I hate myself, and I don't want to inflict any more pain on you. I've destroyed everything."

"You are talking crazy. Stop it," she cried. "This doesn't have to be over."

"Lisa, my father did all of this. He womanized. He drank, and it only got worse. He started hitting my mother, and he beat her up so many times. I know he did it, but she would never say he did. She didn't know what I saw – all the time I saw him beat her. There were times he'd turn on me; she didn't know. I didn't tell her. But one night, I saw them take her away in an ambulance barely breathing. I have to stop this now. I won't go down that path. I have to find a way to fix myself so this doesn't happen. I will not become him." Tom had growled that last sentence with his jaw clenched and eyebrows narrowed.

He stopped for a minute and gazed at her.

"I haven't hit you, Lisa. I promised myself I'd never do that, but I don't understand all of these emotions. I thought I'd locked them all away. I thought I could control them. I also promised I'd never cheat on you. I broke one promise, and I've got to leave you before I break the other promise as well. I could never forgive myself for that."

Lisa backed away and stared at him. She didn't know this man. This was not the man she'd spent more than 27 years of her life with. He was always so even-keeled. He rarely became agitated much less angry. Where was that beautiful smile of his, the one that reassured her it was going to be okay?

"I want to help you, Tom. Please let me help you."

"Lisa, do you know how many women have come on to me

over the years? Do you know how many times I've remembered my mother and what he did to her and restrained myself because I didn't want to be him? Why this time? How did this woman get to me? How did I let my walls down? How did she get under my skin? I have to find out these answers, and I won't drag you down into it. I've done things I never thought I'd do. What's next?"

"Tom, I love you."

"I know you do, and I've done the one thing I vowed never to do to you. I will not go the way of that man, and I can't be with you until I find out why I'm turning into him. I'm going to find a small apartment near the office. I can't lose the business. I may have lost the biggest contract of my life."

Tom walked out of the living room and headed into the bedroom. He pulled a suitcase out from the closet and began putting things in it. Lisa followed. She stood and stared at him. She didn't know what to do. The one remaining piece of her life was slipping out of her grasp. She felt everything crashing down around her. She wanted to cry; she couldn't. She felt numb; this couldn't really be happening. She was in shock.

Tom's cell phone rang.

"Yes. Yes, I know her leaving so abruptly damages the future of the project," he said. "I am aware. I am going to London to meet with her supervisors and the investors tomorrow. Yes, I agree."

He had a grim expression on his face as he ended the call.

"I don't want to go to London, but I have to patch up the damage Christine's return will cause. Gene is going with me. He will be there the entire time. I've told him not to let me out of his sight," he said.

Gene was Kathy's husband, and Tom's first vice-president in charge of marketing and development. He'd worked for Tom since the early days of Tom's company.

With his suitcases packed, Tom headed for the door; he paused to speak to Lisa one last time.

"I'd tell you that I love you, but I don't think you'd believe me at this point. Let me discover why I'm acting this way. Give me some time."

Tom reached out to touch Lisa's face. As his fingers brushed across her cheek, she saw tears in his eyes.

Tom drove to Gene's.

"You drive," he said to Gene.

"Do you want to talk about it?" Gene asked.

"No" came his curt response.

On the long trip to London, Tom ordered several drinks. Gene looked at him. He'd never seen Tom drink and was surprised as how much liquor he was consuming.

"You don't think you've had enough?"

Tom responded with an icy stare. His jaw was clenched as he responded in a threatening tone.

"You just remember who signs your paycheck."

He turned away and stared into the darkness outside the window. Gene didn't say much for the remainder of the flight. Instead, he silently prayed. Tom closed his eyes and tried to sleep.

As if watching a young woman with her whole life in front of her die right before his eyes wasn't horrible enough, the incident had triggered a flood of those memories that he'd tried to forget all of those years. He'd read lots of self-help books, and he thought he had a handle on them. But they erupted in his mind, and like fiery lava, they spilled out into every area of his life. The most vivid memory was of the last time he saw his father. He awoke many nights in a cold sweat as he dreamed of the night, and it was at the forefront of his mind during most of the day. Tom was 9 at the time. His father had come home drunk and started hitting his mother and yelling at her. Tom was awakened to his mother's chilling screams and her begging his father to stop.

"Marvin, I'm sorry. Please stop," Tom could hear his mother pleading.

"Do you want to keep lying to me?" he growled.

"I'm not lying. I'm sorry. I'll do better next time. I promise.

Please."

His mother was sobbing as she choked out the words. He heard the sound of his father's hand hitting his mother repeatedly. Then, there was nothing. No more cries, no whimpers.

Tom knew had to do something. He climbed out of his first-floor window and went next door to ask the neighbors to call the police. They didn't answer the doorbell so Tom beat on it.

"Help me," he yelled.

When his elderly neighbor opened the door, he begged her.

"You gotta call the police," said Tom as he brushed away his tears. "He's killing my mom."

She let Tom in, and her husband called the police. They'd done it before, but they were afraid of Tom's dad too. He'd threatened them for calling the police. When the police arrived, his mother always had an excuse for her bloody nose or black eye. The police knew what was going on, but there was little they could do since his mother refused to press charges.

"Stay here until the police come. Okay," his grandmotherly neighbor said. She tried to smile at Tom. It wasn't long before he heard sirens and saw a mix of red and blue lights. Tom rushed out the front door of the neighbors' house. He watched the police place cuffs on his father. He'd gone into the front yard when he heard the sirens. He was yelling at the police to leave him alone and get off his property. This time his mother couldn't say it was all a misunderstanding. Tom rushed up to the door of his house. He saw blood on the floor, and the paramedics hovering over his mother. Tom watched the paramedics put his mother's limp body onto a gurney. Her eyes were swollen shut, and there was blood on her face. He cried as they put her in the back of the ambulance and ran after them.

"That's my mom. I have to go with her," Tom yelled as one of the police officers grabbed him and kept him from the ambulance.

"Son, you can't go with her," he said as they watched the ambulance pull away.

"She's dead!" Tom screamed.

The officer knelt in front of Tom and looked him in the eye.

"No, son, she's not dead, but she's hurt really bad," he said. "The doctors are going to take care of her."

His neighbor walked over.

"He can stay with us tonight," she said.

"Do you know if there is any other family?" the officer asked.

"The little boy's grandmother is about an hour away."

Tom was jolted from his sleep.

That was his scariest memory, but it unlocked a multitude of other memories of screams and pleas for mercy. Tom had peeked through his bedroom door on many nights to see what was happening; the helpless feeling overwhelmed him. He had tried to stop his father once, but his father was a big man. He threw the little boy across the room and told him he'd kill him if Tom ever tried to stop him again. Tom knew he would have kept that promise. Close to 40 years of anger was built up inside of him, but the flood of ignored emotions was too much for him to bear. He had to deal with them somehow.   But how?

He flagged the flight attendant and ordered another Scotch.

Gene pretended to be asleep. He silently prayed for wisdom to help his friend.

5

The antique grandfather clock in the hallway was the only sound in the house. In the few days since Tom's confession and departure, she barely moved from the spot on the floor of her bedroom, where she'd collapsed in a heap of tears after he'd left. The monotonous clicks and hourly chimes had been her only company. Lisa had never realized how loud the ticking was, but it became deafening, almost torturous at times. She wasn't sure what she felt - numb; angry; hopeless; depressed – all of them yet none of them. She thought she'd felt empty before. She thought there was nothing left inside until the reality of Tom's infidelity hit her.

Tom had never talked about his father. She only brought up the subject once. His expression turned cold and steely, and in a low, but menacing tone, he told her he didn't have a father and never to mention it again. It was the only time in their marriage she was afraid of Tom. Then as if nothing had happened, he smiled and started talking about something else. She wasn't sure if Tom's father had died or if he was still alive. She had only met his mother, a frail woman who spent a lot of time in the hospital. She looked much older than she was, and she died just a few years after Tom and Lisa were married. An aneurism ultimately killed her, but Lisa wondered. She suspected her mother-in-law and Tom had been abused because of Tom's reaction. There were also looks on his mother's face at times. Lisa had never really asked many questions about her mother-in-law's illnesses;

he was touchy when it came to that. Lisa wondered if the years of abuse at the hands of Tom's father were something his mother never healed from. Tom was overprotective of her, and Lisa had thought it was sweet. But now that Lisa was older than her mother-in-law was at the time of her death, Lisa wondered about so many things. She didn't feel she even knew her own husband. He had dark secrets he never opened up to her about. There was more to his betrayal than his time with Christine.

She remembered her chance encounter with the old fisherman. He said it would be okay. Could she believe the random words of a stranger? And what did Tom mean about a text? She hadn't sent one on the night he didn't come home.

At times, she'd doze off. When she did, she'd see herself in African villages, rocking sick babies. She knew they were infected with HIV or some other disease. Even the older children were tiny, frail and malnourished. After she opened her eyes, she could still see them.

Maybe things weren't as bad for her as she thought.

As she pondered, she heard the doorbell, and then someone beating on the door.

"Lisa," a voice called. "Are you in there? Answer the door."

Lisa couldn't feel her legs. She'd been in one position for so long. She didn't know if she could move.

"Lisa!" the voice continued.

It sounded like Kathy. Lisa managed to stand and walked slowly to the door. Kathy continued to beat on the door.   Lisa unlocked the kitchen door and let her in.

"Lisa, you look like death," said Kathy.

"Thanks. Great to see you too," Lisa replied as she closed the door behind Kathy.

"I've been so worried about you. Why haven't you been answering your phone?"

"Because I don't want to talk to anyone."

"Gene told me everything, and he said Tom looks like death too."

"I'm glad to hear it," Lisa said without emotion.

"Is there anything I can do?"

"No, there's nothing. I just want to be left alone. Please, Kathy."

"Have you eaten anything since he left?"

Lisa shook her head and sat down at the kitchen table. Kathy stared at the grocery bags Lisa had hastily left on the counter when she found Tom home early.

"How long have these been sitting here?" Kathy asked. She opened a milk carton. After sniffing it, she immediately proceeded to dump the liquid down the sink.

"I don't know. What day is it? They've been there since Tom left."

"That's been two days."

"Then, it's been two days."

"I knew I should have come over yesterday especially since you weren't answering your phone."

Kathy looked in the rest of the bags.

"All of this is going to have to be thrown out."

Lisa nodded. Kathy looked in the refrigerator to make something for Lisa to eat.

"Don't bother. I'm not hungry."

"You have to eat something. I take it you haven't eaten since Tom and Gene left?"

"No, I'm not hungry."

Kathy found a can of chicken noodle soup in the cupboard and opened it. She continued to talk as she prepared the soup, but Lisa wasn't really paying attention. She stared at the table. She felt like she was a character in an unending nightmare.

Kathy placed the bowl in front of Lisa and sat down. Lisa pushed it away.

"Gene said they will be in London two or three weeks or possibly longer," said Kathy, pushing the soup back to her. "This whole Christine thing has thrown a wrench into the business deal."

"I'm so sorry they might lose a business deal. After all, business is the most important thing here," Lisa pushed the soup away from her.

"I'm sorry. That's not how I meant it."

"This whole Christine thing has thrown a wrench into my life. And what difference does it make anyway? Tom wasn't" Lisa stopped mid-sentence.

"Planning on coming back?" Kathy finished the sentence.

Lisa nodded as she looked at the table.

"Lisa, I know you love him. I know you have stuck beside him in many bad times. I wouldn't give up on him just yet."

"I'm not the one who gave up. He did when he walked out the door."

"Don't give up on living and don't give up on Tom yet. I believe he loves you. Gene said he's been miserable since they left. He hasn't eaten or slept."

"Well that makes two of us."

"And don't block out real friends."

"I'll try to remember that," Lisa said. "But I don't know who my real friends are. I don't even know who my husband is anymore."

Kathy reached out across the table to touch her friend's hand. She squeezed it and smiled at Lisa.

"Tom has been trying to call you. Gene said he's probably tried hundreds of times in the past couple of days."

"I don't want to talk to him right now," Lisa said and shook her head. "I told you I don't want to talk to anyone."

Kathy walked back to the island where Lisa's purse had spilled out. She picked up Lisa's phone. It was dead.

"Where's your charger?" Kathy asked.

"Bedroom."

Kathy walked to Lisa's bedroom and brought her charger back. She plugged the phone in and placed it in front of Lisa.

Lisa stared at the phone. Two to three weeks, Lisa thought. That was approaching Thanksgiving. How was she going to explain this to Brittany and Spencer? How was she going to explain this to anyone? She wasn't sure she wanted to plug in the phone. She knew she couldn't talk to Tom. What would she say with him across the Atlantic Ocean?

"I don't want to talk to Tom."

"I know you don't, honey, but you need to."

Lisa shook her head.

"I gave you all the time I'm going to give you," said Kathy. "Maybe I should have come over sooner. I didn't know what to do."

"I don't think I'll be up to social visits for a while. My life is over. My kids are gone. I have no job. I've been married to a man I don't even know. I have no purpose for even being here anymore."

Lisa placed her elbows on the table and buried her face in her hands. She wanted to stop thinking and stop feeling.

"Lisa, don't say things like that."

"It's true."

Lisa folded her hands in front of her, and Kathy pushed her phone into Lisa's hands.

"No, call Tom. I'm here for you. I promise. I'm only a phone call away," Kathy said.

Kathy gave her a brief hug. She turned on Lisa's phone. When she did, it sprang to life with a slew of text and voicemail messages. Lisa stared at it as Kathy left. Her voice mail was full. Most of them were from Tom, who sounded like she felt, empty and dead. News had gotten around fast. There were a couple of messages from people obviously wanting more information and juicy details to pass on. Lisa did a lot of volunteer work for local arts groups. Her children had been heavily involved, but with them gone, Lisa had made it clear she wanted to take some time off. She didn't even finish listening to a couple of them before she deleted them, but one of them did catch her attention.

"Hey, lady. This is Jessie. I have something you might be interested in. I'm not sure. It's writing-related, but it requires some travel – extensive travel. Anyway, give me a buzz, and I'll give you the details."

Writing-related and extensive travel. Anything to get her present worries off her mind and to stop her from thinking about missions work in Africa. She didn't want to go to Africa – not now. Those dreams were long dead. It was too late.

Despite listening to the clock chime every hour on the hour, Lisa had no idea what time it was. She glanced at her phone. It was 6:30, but Jessie would probably still be in the office. She worked a lot of early evenings.

"Jessie. I figured you'd still be in the office."

"I'm headed out to a rehearsal in a few minutes. The River Theatre is doing Rodgers and Hammerstein again and without you this time. How are you holding up? I heard about Tom."

"Is there anyone in this town who hasn't heard about Tom?"

"I do have my fingers on the pulse of this community, my dear, and your involvement with the arts has placed you in the artery."

"I'm numb," said Lisa. "I don't know how I am, but writing sounds like what I need."

"This is different. It happened to cross my desk. There's a non-profit in town that works with some area churches, and they banded together to raise money for a well-drilling truck. They've got the truck, and they are sending it into Africa."

Lisa's mouth dropped at the mention of the continent. She felt her knees weakening as she slowly sunk to the floor. It couldn't be possible.

"Did you say 'Africa?'"

"Yes, is there something wrong?"

"No, no, go ahead."

"Anyway, a group of them is going over there between Thanksgiving and Christmas. Then, another group is going back after Christmas to stay for about two months."

"Okay so what's that got to do with me?" Lisa asked.

"It's a heartwarming story, and they want to do something

with it. One of the pastors is also trying to get an orphanage and school built. They want a writer to go with them. Listen, it's not going to pay a lot from what I can tell. I'm not really sure of the details on that. I can't imagine they'd have much money to pay you at all. In fact, you would probably have to buy your plane ticket, but they said they'd take care of the rest. They want the proceeds from sales of a book to go toward the future mission projects. Also, the paper is interested in something too, and James said they may be able to wiggle a little bit in the budget to get something out. They want photos from Africa, and some first-hand accounts. You know they can't afford to send anyone, but if someone is there, apparently, they can justify a budget waiver. Besides, there's a wealthy business owner on the board of this thing. I'm not sure why he's so gung-ho, but he's a crony of the publisher and has agreed to throw some big bucks on additional advertising if we will play this one."

Jessie paused.

"I'm not really sure why I called you, but James and I were talking about it. I'm taking on some of the assignment editor's jobs these days with the budget cuts and all. You were the first person who popped into our heads. He would have called, but they are in department head meetings this week discussing next year's budget."

"I think I know why you called," Lisa said as she grabbed a piece of paper and a pen from her purse which was on the island in the kitchen. She couldn't stray too far from the leash of her phone's power cord. "Who's the contact?"

"The pastor in charge is named Matthew Davis; he's also over the non-profit. I'll send you an email with his number and a link to the website."

"That would be great. I'll definitely give him a call."

"Great! Let us know what you come up with, and Lisa, if there's anything else I can do, let me know."

Lisa tried to produce a weak laugh.

"I know better than to trust a reporter."

Jessie laughed.

"I'm not the society columnist so don't worry."

"I know. Besides, I've known you long enough to trust you. I just don't think I could handle you telling me 'I told you so.'"

"I wouldn't ever do that to you, Lisa. You mean too much to me."

"Thanks, Jessie, because you were right."

"That wasn't something I ever wanted to be right about."

Lisa hung up the phone. She couldn't call the pastor until the morning. She wasn't sure what to do, but all of a sudden she felt a surge of energy and saw a flicker of hope. A couple of months ago, she might have used the word "coincidental" to describe what she was going through, but it seemed more than that. Divine providence maybe?

She walked into the living room. There was a large built-in bookcase with lots of books. There were many antique volumes that Lisa had in the room because she thought they added a little bit of charm, but now, she was looking for one book in particular that had been gathering dust for years.

"God, my life is a mess. I don't want to live like this anymore. I'm sorry for all the wasted years. I have nothing left except my ability to write and a heart that is willing, but I'll give You what I have. If You can make anything of it, go ahead," she whispered as she pulled the book off the shelf.

She flipped open the pages, and her eyes fell on Gen.12:1, where she saw God tell Abram to get out of his family's house and go to a land He would show him.

Lisa felt a chill. That seemed to be speaking to her. Could this assignment be an open door? She closed the Bible.

This was crazy to her. She couldn't run off to Africa - or could she?

She thumbed through some more pages and found another scripture underlined. "Love never fails."

Lisa took a deep breath. It sure looked like it was failing right now. Their love was undergoing the ultimate test. Would it survive?

She hoped so.

Another book also caught her eye. It was her Shakespeare textbook from college. Her college minor was English. She almost majored in it, but she got into the journalism track instead. One of her favorite English courses was the one on Shakespeare. She loved listening to her professor read the Bard in his British accent. She sighed at the memory. The thick red volume on her shelf contained all of Shakespeare's plays and sonnets. She flipped through its worn pages. She'd read those poems many times over the years. There was a handmade bookmark stuck in its pages. She'd doodled Tom's name in various shades of ink. One of the sonnets was highlighted in yellow. It was Sonnet 116 about unfailing love.

"O no! it is an ever-fixed mark

That looks on tempests and is never shaken;"

She stared at the words; the passage sounded familiar. Love not failing; love not being shaken. She was looking at the tempest, but she was so unsure. Was Shakespeare right? Could love survive all storms? She remembered the fisherman who had told her that things would be okay. Was her love strong enough to pull her through? Was Tom's?

She realized she still had messages to check. There were several from Tom asking her to call when she got the message. He sounded tired and anxious. His voice was tortured. While she wanted to talk to him, listening to his messages sent daggers into her heart. She scrolled through the text messages. Most of them said the same thing as his voicemail messages. Since her voicemail was full, and she hadn't responded, she could tell he was upset. She didn't know what to do. She fought the urge to call him back or text him. What would she say to him? She'd spent the last few days playing out conversations with him in her mind. In some, she lashed out; in others, she tried to understand. She didn't want to roll over and give up on more than half of her life she'd spent with him. She stared at the cell phone. What time was it in England? As she stared at it, the phone began to ring. It was Tom. She wasn't sure she wanted to answer it.

Her aching heart began to pound.

"Hello," she said in a hoarse whisper.

"Hey Angel, I was worried about you."

"I'm fine," she came back in a clipped tone.

There was a pause.

"I know you aren't fine," said Tom. "I've been calling since I left. You haven't answered the phone, and you haven't responded to my texts. I've been worried. I've handled this all wrong. I've handled everything wrong. I'm going to have to be in England for several weeks. It could run into Thanksgiving. It's just another day over here. It could take longer."

"I know. Kathy came by. You wanted time apart, to figure things out. And you got it."

Lisa was surprised at how cold that sounded when it left her lips. Tom must have been too. He didn't say anything. The awkward pause grew until he cleared his throat.

"You'll be glad to know Gene is with me, and he's agreed to stay the entire time."

"Tom, I've always trusted you. It's you who doesn't trust you. I don't need a spy. I've never spied on you. I won't live my life worried about what you are doing and with whom. I love you, and I always will. I'm not the one who left."

"I didn't mean to hurt you. I'm trying to make this right, and if I get this contract, there is the possibility of another one on its heels."

"Do what you need to do. I don't have much of a life so I'm sure I'll still be here when you decide."

"I'll call you and keep you up to date. Please don't stop answering your phone again," he said. "I need to hear your voice."

She didn't answer because she knew she would say something she'd regret.

"And Lisa, I do love you. Please believe me."

"I'm sure it's late over there, Tom. You should probably get some rest. Good night, Tom."

After she hung up the phone, that sense of numbness returned. It all seemed surreal. Did he leave her? What had happened over the past few days? It was only 7:30. It was too early to go to bed although that's all she could think about doing. Sleep to escape everything going on around her.

She walked back into their bedroom. Memories hit her as soon as she walked in. They'd lived in the same house for 15 years. There were many romantic nights they'd spent together. She couldn't sleep in there. Too many emotions. The kids' rooms brought a different kind of pain. It was back to the living room. The couch there was comfortable enough. She didn't think she'd be able to sleep anyway. She decided to mindlessly flip through television stations. As she clicked, she saw one of those infomercials for a world hunger relief program with their heartbreaking photos of starving children.

"Of course, you are in Africa," Lisa spoke to the television as she turned it off. "That figures."

She leaned back against the pillows and pulled one over her face.

"God, do You really want me to go to Africa? How can I go to Africa and still make my marriage work?"

6

Gene watched Tom's expressions as he talked to Lisa. He saw a range of emotions in the few minutes. When he called her "angel," there was a soft smile which quickly melted at what had to have been a brusque response. There were a few times that his expression shattered as though he'd been kicked in the stomach. When he told Lisa he loved her, there was a deep pain evident in his eyes.

He was silent as he hung up the phone. He sat on the edge of the couch with his elbows on his knees, and his hands folded as if he were praying. He closed his eyes and leaned his head against his hands for a few minutes before getting up and heading to the bottle of Scotch. Gene had stayed quiet while he searched for the right words to say. He walked over to Tom and put his hand on the bottle.

"This isn't helping you." Gene said.

"Please, Gene, leave me alone. What did I tell you?"

Tom's voice was hoarse, and he sounded as though he was struggling to hold back tears. Tom glared at Gene.

Gene knew what had taken place with Tom and Christine, but other than a brief confession from Tom with a plea for Gene to accompany him to London, Tom had said nothing else. In fact, Tom had said very little other than business-related conversation since they'd left the states. Gene had waited for Tom to open up, but it was obvious Tom wasn't going to say anything without some prompting.

"I'm sorry, but you didn't bring me along for me to leave you alone." Gene said. "And you can fire me. I don't care. You are more important to me than a job."

Tom looked startled. He walked over to the window and turned his back to Gene. He felt vulnerable, and he didn't want anyone to see him like that, not even Gene, who was the closest thing he had to a best friend.

"Why did you tell Lisa?" Gene asked him.

Tom turned to look at Gene. He narrowed his eyes and had an incredulous look on his face.

"Why wouldn't I? I tell Lisa everything," he said. "The thing is I didn't have to tell her. She already knew. She told me she already knew."

Tom shook his head, seemingly unable to comprehend how she could have known.

"No, you don't."

"I don't what?"

"You don't tell her everything. Why didn't you tell her you were fighting these feelings? Why didn't you take her into your arms and erase all thoughts of another woman before anything ever happened between you and Christine? This didn't just happen. There were thoughts and events that led up to it. And those of us watching could see the signs."

Tom looked down. The thought had never occurred to him.

"What about this drinking? You've never been a drinker. What feelings are you trying to escape? Why have you shut Lisa out?" Gene asked.

"I don't know."

Tom sat down and buried his head in his hands.

"Tom, I keep quiet about things, and maybe, I shouldn't. We've worked so closely together over the years. I think of you as my friend rather than my boss. I should have said something to you, warned you, but I didn't think you'd fall for this. I've watched you blow off other women with so much skill they didn't know what happened to them," Gene said.

Tom nodded.

"And you of all people should know I'm a man of faith. I haven't tried to push anything on you."

"Yes, I've respected you for that."

"Well, it's time I spoke to you about it. It's my relationship with God that keeps me from doing anything to hurt Kathy. I won't say I would never do what you've done, but I pray every day to keep myself only for Kathy. It's hard sometimes not to think about what it would be like to be with someone else. You send me out of town enough. I'm aware of the temptations that are out there. We have many beautiful women in our office. I get lonely at times."

"Why are you telling me this?"

"Because no one else is close enough to you, and I'm willing to lose my job over it. I'm willing to lose a friend if I have to, but it has to be said to you. When I met you, you and Lisa went to church. There was a basis of faith in your marriage, and the only thing that will restore your marriage and make it better is a relationship with God. He can also heal the broken little boy inside of you who was abused by his father."

"Never mention my father." Tom stood as he raised his voice and pointed at Gene. "Never."

"You told me you didn't want to be like him. Until you can be healed from what he did to you and your mother, you will never be free from his shadow and his influence. And we have to address this drinking problem you have. I won't say anything more to you tonight, but I'm on a mission to see you and Lisa put back together. Lisa has many great qualities. She's compassionate and kind, and you are one lucky man to have her. If you don't repair this, another man will come along and treat her with the respect she deserves. Most importantly, I'm on a mission to see you whole. As I see it, we've got a lot of time together over the next few weeks, and you are stuck with me. I know you won't send me home, and I know you will still sign my paycheck. I don't know what has caused this, but I know I have not seen the man I've known and respected for the past 20 years in the past few months. I'm determined to see him come back, and I'll do everything in my power to make that happen. The great thing is that I know a higher power, and He loves you. "

Gene stood up and walked to the door of his room. He turned for a brief second before closing the door and saw Tom standing staring with a shocked expression. No one talked to Tom like that. Tom smiled at Gene and gave him a mock salute.

"I'm glad I brought you along, and I promise not to fire you – not today anyway."

Tom slowly returned to his seat.

He realized he was stinging from the words both Lisa and Gene had said, and he knew there was truth in what both of them had said. He always turned to Lisa, except when it came to his relationship with his father. Now, he locked her out of this too. He didn't want out of the marriage. He didn't want to be with Christine. Why now? Things weren't bad between Lisa and him before. One thing Lisa said stood out. Tom didn't trust himself. Christine was in the same city, working for the same firm he was trying to finalize the details of the contract with. He had gone to London in hopes of working with someone else. He couldn't trust himself around her after what had happened. That's the reason Gene was there.

Since arriving in London, he'd seen Christine in the office. She wasn't working on the deal, but he was aware of her presence. He was fighting the attraction he had to her; he was fighting a whole range of unfamiliar emotions. Tom stared out the window of his room overlooking London while a battle raged in his mind. Where did it all go wrong? He wasn't sure. Maybe it wasn't just one day and one event. Gene was right.

He remembered the first time Christine had come into his office. She was blonde and beautiful, and she knew it. She dressed to flaunt every womanly attribute, and men's heads turned when she entered a room. He knew she used her charm to put business deals together in her favor. Over the course of the next few weeks, they'd spent a lot of time working out details on this particular project. She had made it clear she was a single woman who liked the company of men, but she was too busy for "emotional entanglements" as she called them. She had her career first. In her mid-20s, she felt like she had plenty of time later to settle down and have a family. Young men bored her, she said. She liked men with status and what she perceived as class. When she wanted something, she went after it, and she made it clear she wanted Tom. She was different from Lisa. He couldn't deny she was attractive to him, but he tried to keep his guard up.

One night after everyone had left the office, Tom lingered. He was so close to sealing up all the details on this deal. If he could just make it a few more days, he'd be home free. It was something about the time of year. He could feel fall in the air at night on some of those otherwise hot Georgia days. He knew that his father had gone to jail in the fall. He remembered a slight chill in the air as he ran through the neighbor's yard in his bare feet so late at night. His neighbor's door had a wreath with gold, orange and red leaves as well as miniature pumpkins on it. He remembered looking up at it as he banged on the door.

Tom wished he could get those images out of his head. Since they'd come out like a flood, he saw that day in his mind all the time. He sat in the dark at his desk and grabbed the bottle of Scotch from the bottom drawer. Maybe, if he got the deal signed in the next few days, he could take a vacation with Lisa to somewhere far away. Maybe, he could forget it again. Why was he remembering all of this now? Then, he saw Courtney's face. He wanted to scream.

He'd had several glasses of alcohol when he heard a voice cut through the darkness.

"Drinking alone?"

It was Christine.

"That's the only way I drink," he replied.

"It's much more fun with someone else."

"I don't drink for fun."

She turned on one of the lights. She was wearing a mini-skirt and tight-fitting button-up blouse. She held a bottle in one hand and walked toward him.

"I'll be leaving in a few days, and I'd like to have a little fun before I do," she said as she sat on his desk.

"I told you you are barking up the wrong tree."

She smiled.

"I've never had anyone play 'hard to get' so long. You have been quite a challenge. One I've enjoyed."

"Christine, I'm sorry. I can't do this. I can't do this to my wife," he said.

He tried to stand up. He wanted to leave the office. He'd had too much Scotch. He felt dizzy.

Christine laughed.

"You wouldn't be doing anything to your wife." she said as she began to unbutton her blouse. "Besides, she doesn't need to know."

He picked up his jacket and started for the door, but she blocked him.

"You are in no condition to drive home, Tommy. You are quite drunk," she said as she grabbed his tie and pulled her to him. She kissed him passionately, and he responded. He knew he was too weak to fight it any longer.

Around 4 a.m., he heard his phone. He had a couch and several chairs in his office. He was lying on the couch. He looked around for Christine; she was gone, but he could still smell her perfume in the air. He remembered very little up to that point. All he kept seeing in his mind was the crushed look he knew Lisa would have when he told her what he'd done. He got dressed and found his phone. There was a text from Lisa. It said "I love you, and I miss you." He felt ill and not just from all the liquor he'd consumed.

He locked himself in his office and left a message on his secretary's desk to hold all calls and cancel all meetings. He didn't want to be disturbed by anyone including his wife or Christine. He kept a spare suit in his office, and he changed into it. He had a small bathroom in his office. He splashed water onto his face and then he stared at himself in the mirror. He'd forgotten his father's face in the multitude of memories he'd forced deep into his soul, but there staring back at him was the man he hated so much. He walked over to his desk. She'd left an extra bottle of Scotch on his desk. It was half empty. How much did they drink? He held the bottle in his hands and stared at it. He wanted to pour another one, and he wasn't sure he could resist the urge.

Lisa's text turned out to be a random glitch. Several of Lisa's messages from days before had flooded his phone. He only noticed the one telling him she loved him. It only reinforced the guilt and shame he felt. That night might have been the culmination of things, but his betrayal of Lisa began earlier. As he sat in that London room, Tom thought about the dinners with Christine and their conversations about their pasts. He opened up to her about what he was going through about things he hadn't told Lisa about. He talked to Christine about his parents and the abuse. He had gotten emotionally involved with Christine during that time. Why didn't he tell Lisa? Why did he think she would judge him for his father? It was easy to talk to Christine. Surely, it would have been easy to talk to Lisa. It had always been so easy to talk to Lisa. As he wrestled with thoughts, he knew he wasn't going to be able to sleep, but he couldn't remember the last time he slept.

At their house, Lisa couldn't sleep either. She was awake and off the couch at 5 a.m. She couldn't get the images of the children in Africa out of her brain. When she drifted off to sleep, she saw their faces. She saw herself feeding them and caring for them. In between the vision of her helping children, she saw Tom and Christine; her mind conjured up pictures she didn't want to see. Her numbness gave way to her pain and anger. She didn't think she had many tears left to cry, but she was surprised as the emotion forced its way out of her.

After several hours of nonstop crying, she managed to compose herself long enough to call Rev. Davis and set up an appointment with him to talk about the project. He was available later in the morning. She needed a distraction, and this would be a huge one for her. Deep inside though, she thought it could be more than a distraction, maybe, it could bring purpose back into her life.

Her biggest concern was the timing of the trip. In a way, it was perfect. She could leave the house and all of the reminders of Tom and their life together. It all seemed like such a lie. But it was at Thanksgiving. How could she leave at Thanksgiving? And what was she going to tell the kids about her and Tom? He was in London on business. That was a good excuse not to have to tell them anything for a couple of weeks at least. Christmas was usually the big celebration with extended family. Thanksgiving was low-key with the children only.

Lisa forced herself to take a shower and change her clothes. She'd worn the same thing since Tom had left. She went into the kitchen. She should make herself eat. The soup was still on the table from where she'd left it untouched the night before. She moved slowly around the kitchen, opening cabinet doors and standing in front of the refrigerator. Nothing appealed to her. She decided to leave without eating.

The drive to Rev. Davis' Christ Church took about 20 minutes. She created a list of questions to ask. She had a pad and pen ready to take as many notes as possible. She would do this under the guise of trying to make an informed decision, but she already knew in her heart she was going to Africa. She didn't think she could talk herself out of it.

The pastor's secretary showed her in. Not only was the Rev. Davis waiting, but she recognized Grayson Devereux, who must have been the benefactor Jessie Rose had mentioned in their conversation. Mr. Devereux was in his late 60s and was indeed a close friend of the newspaper publisher. She was one of the few newspaper reporters in town that he liked because the only time he saw her was when she was covering some type of happening related to his benevolence. Other reporters got on his bad side. He'd had his share of controversy. He was accused of having several city officials in his back pocket. Nothing could ever be proven, and with the publisher of the newspaper on his side, nothing negative was ever written about him. That didn't prevent television and radio news from pursuing him, but so much of it was hearsay. They couldn't find any true dirt on him either. She was surprised to find him there with such short notice on their meeting. She knew he was an extremely busy man. This project must be very important, she thought.

"Ah, Lisa Kinsey, my favorite reporter, so good to see you," Mr. Devereux stood as she entered. He firmly grasped her hand. "I'm glad someone still listens to me in this town."

She knew he must have been talking about the paper's publisher and her editors.

She shook Rev. Davis' hand as well.

"I see you've met Mr. Devereux," he said.

"Of course. Who hasn't?"

"Lisa, I'm glad to have you on with this project. You see - my son, after many years of squandering my money on drugs and less than desirable women has finally settled down with a solid woman of impeccable character. He's a reformed man. She was in the Peace Corps for several years and saw the plight of these African villages which have had no rain. I want my son to look like a saint and not the scandalous party boy he once was. Rev. Davis here is my daughter-in-law's brother, and he also shares her concern, not necessarily mine."

Lisa smiled and nodded as Mr. Devereux stole the Rev. Davis' thunder.

"So we put together a group of churches and created a non-profit. Now you need to tell their story. And Lisa, I will make sure that everything you need will be taken care of. The newspaper will quietly back this project with its printing and staffing resources because I'm behind them with the checkbook."

Lisa understood completely.

Now it was Rev. Davis' turn.

"I know we haven't formally asked you to do this. Do you have any questions before we do? I know the timing of the trip is awkward, but there are many committed people on board. Some of them are only going to a week, but there are several who are staying the entire time. And Mr. Devereux wanted to get this going before the end of the year," said the Rev. Davis, who was in his early 30s with blonde hair and a tan even in October. He looked and sounded more like a California surfer than a pastor.

"We have this drilling machine to dig wells. There are places in Africa that haven't had rain in years. The river beds are completely dry. My daughter-in-law saw it firsthand. We have a team in place that is permanently there. They will do the actual drilling, but we need to send in support teams. All of these people are from this area. They've all come together to help, and they know their money is going directly to help -not to some international foreign aid organization," Mr. Devereux interjected.

When he got behind a project with his money and his mouth, Mr. Devereux was someone people did not want to tangle with. He had a lot of energy. All of a sudden, Lisa saw Tom sitting there instead of Mr. Devereux. There were a few times when Tom got on board with a project. She remembered when one of the smaller community theater organizations needed a new location for its performances. It had been using a school auditorium, but the group needed a permanent home because the school was being torn down. Spencer and Lisa had been in several plays there, and Tom had watched Spencer come into his own after being on stage. Eventually, they found an old movie theater and turned it into a dinner theater. Tom spent countless hours rallying support and raising money. She was so proud to be Tom's wife during that time.

Lisa realized she'd missed some of the conversation.

"So what exactly do you have in mind for me?" Lisa asked.

"You are going to document this for us, my dear," said Mr. Devereux. "We want newspaper articles, a book, a website, lots of publicity. Also, we want my foundation to be mentioned. And as I said, I will take care of everything for you. Nothing shows people have changed better than sending them to an impoverished nation and making them do something good for someone for a change."

"Do you have a passport?" asked Rev. Davis.

Lisa nodded.

"You will need some extra shots too," he said. "Oh, and I don't know the dates they told you, but we leave the Tuesday before Thanksgiving. We plan to drill wells in a few villages before coming back. Also, there is a construction group going to build a small school and orphanage. The really cool thing about this project is how people from several different denominations, ethnic groups and communities are coming together to see this project through."

She could tell she was going to like this Rev. Davis. He spoke with such exuberance it was contagious.

"Well, it's settled. Lisa, my secretary will be in touch," said Mr. Devereux as he rose from his chair. He shook the pastor's hand and Lisa's. "If you will excuse me, I have a meeting with the mayor."

Lisa turned to go, but the Rev. Davis stopped her.

"Can you stay for a few more minutes?"

"Sure."

"Do you mind if I call you Lisa?" he asked.

"No, that's fine," she said.

"I know Mr. Devereux means well. At least, I keep telling myself that. He's been a huge help. His son is a great guy underneath it all or else I wouldn't have let my sister marry him."

Lisa and Rev. Davis both laughed.

"We have a meeting of the team a week from Sunday evening at 6. It will be here if you'd like to come and meet everyone."

"That would be great. I will be here."

She turned to leave.

"I need to ask you a personal question. Are you a woman of faith?"

Lisa paused. She wasn't sure how to answer that question. She was so confused.

"I was at one time. I don't know what I am now. Does it matter?"

"For your part in this, no, it doesn't. I was just asking."

Lisa laughed and shook her head.

"I can't explain it, but somehow I know I'm supposed to do this. My head tells me I'm crazy, but my gut tells me otherwise."

He nodded.

"I've been on trips to this region several times. I know the people we are going with, and if you aren't a woman of faith now, you probably will be by the time you return. It's not a Sunday only thing for them. They live it, eat it and breathe it. They are passionate about what they do," he said. "I see you are married from your wedding band. What does your husband think about this?"

Lisa winced as she looked down at her left hand to avoid the pastor's stare.

"He's on business in London right now. It's complicated, and he probably won't be back before Christmas," she looked down and turned quickly toward the door.

"Is everything okay?" he asked.

"Yes. It's fine. It's been nice meeting you, and I know I'll be seeing a lot of you soon." She didn't know how much longer she could hold the tears back so she rushed out of the office.

7

Lisa only had a couple of weeks to prepare for the trip. Part of her felt like a teenager plotting to run away from home. She wanted to get away from everything, but she didn't know how to explain it to everyone. The morning after her visit with Rev. Davis and Mr. Devereux, Spencer sent her an email about Thanksgiving. She felt a knot in her stomach as she started to open it. It was brief, but it was like Spencer. He didn't talk much. She was surprised to even hear from him.

"Hey Mom," it read. "With the new job, I don't get too much time off from work. I have to work the day after Thanksgiving so there's no way I can come home. It's not looking good for Christmas either."

Instead of being sad, however, Lisa was almost happy her son wasn't coming home for the holidays. As she was trying to digest that, someone rang the doorbell. It was a flower delivery with an arrangement of two dozen, gorgeous red roses in a crystal vase. The card simply said "I love you, T."

She put them on the island in the center of the kitchen and stared at the vase.

All of a sudden, years of reporter cynicism, lack of sleep and food and more pent-up emotion rushed out of her as she picked the vase and threw it at the wall.

"If you loved me, why did you do this to me?" she screamed

as the vase shattered, and she slid to the floor in a sobbing heap. Lisa wasn't sure how long she lay on the kitchen floor. The release of the emotion caused her to realize how exhausted she was. Maybe she should take a nap. She could clean up the mess later. She began to head for her bed on the living room couch when she heard the buzzing of her vibrating phone on the counter. It was Tom. It wasn't surprising.

"Yes," she answered.

"Hi Angel," he said.

She realized the numbness had now given way to anger. She could only think he was acting like a stereotypical cheater with his hand caught in the cookie jar. She used to love it when he called her "angel;" now it caused her skin to crawl.

"Yes," she tried to calm her voice.

"Did you get the roses?"

"Yes. They arrived a little while ago. I separated them," she paused. "They are all over the kitchen right now. I didn't realize how red roses matched the tile in the kitchen until now."

She almost laughed as she looked at the mess she'd made in her fit of rage. Rose petals, leaves and stems were strewn all over the terra cotta tiles, and the pieces of broken crystal shimmered as the light hit them. She hadn't laughed in several days. She was wondering what was wrong with her. Laughter was so inappropriate, but her emotions were in turmoil. She didn't want to cry any longer, but she had to do something to get all of these feelings out.

"Are you okay?" he asked.

"Sure, I'm doing just great for a woman whose husband has recently admitted he's having an affair and now has gone several thousand miles away from his wife to another country to be closer to this woman he supposedly doesn't care about. I'm doing great, Tom. There, are you happy now?"

The words, dripping with a biting sarcasm, spilled out of her mouth before she had a chance to stop them. They were sharper than the crystal shards which lay on the floor, but they'd been building up inside her. She was surprised she'd kept them in as long as she had.

"I deserve that."

"Yes, you do. I need you, and I need you here. I don't need you in a different time zone. I don't need you trying to figure things out without me. I don't want to argue over the phone."

"I don't want to argue at all."

"We never really have so what's the problem now?"

"I don't know, Lisa, and it scares me. Lots of things scare me right now."

Lisa started to pick up the crystal shards from the vase off the floor. As she picked one of them up, it sliced into her hand and began to bleed. Lisa cried out.

"What's wrong, Lisa?"

"Nothing, Tom," she said as she grabbed a dish cloth and wrapped it around her hand.

"You sound like you are in pain – physical pain."

"I cut myself, and I'm bleeding. I will talk to you later."

She hung up the phone. Lisa had a deep gash in her hand, but at least it was her left hand. She needed her right one. She covered it back and hoped the bleeding would stop. She carefully gathered the rest of the pieces from the vase and threw them away. She salvaged several of the roses and put them into another vase. As she was finishing, she turned to see Kathy coming in the kitchen.

"Really? Does he have you on speed dial? Your husband is babysitting mine. I don't need one too," Lisa said as she looked her hand. It was still bleeding.

"Tom is concerned about you."

"If he was concerned he'd be here, not with his mistress in London," she snapped.

"You know he's not with her."

"I don't know anything, Kathy. He could have been calling me from her room for all I know."

"You've watched way too many talk shows."

"I'm a reporter. I'm paid to be cynical and not trust what

comes out of people's mouths," she started. "What would you think? Your husband tells you he's sleeping with someone else and says he needs time. Then, he's on the next plane to another country where this woman happens to live."

"He's not alone, and you know that."

"Kathy, if Tom decides to see this woman, what is Gene going to do? Is he going to tie Tom to a chair?"

Kathy tried not to laugh at the image Lisa had just painted.

"Put yourself in my position."

"I'm sorry, Lisa."

Kathy took the broom from Lisa to try to recover any more tiny pieces of glass.

"How's the hand?"

"It's still bleeding."

"Come on, let's have it checked out."

"I'm a big girl."

"I know, but you should have it looked at. Besides, your husband signs

my husband's paychecks, and I really like his paychecks."

Lisa laughed.

"Well at least you're honest," Lisa said

Kathy drove Lisa to the nearest clinic and waited for her.

"Mrs. Kinsey, it doesn't appear that you've done any serious damage, but there are a few pieces of glass in your hand, I need to remove," said the doctor.

"I know this isn't a rusty nail, but I probably need to get a tetanus booster. I'm going to Africa soon. Do you give the other shots here?"

"Actually, we have some of the more common ones, but I can refer you to someone. What will you be doing over there?"

She explained a little about the project. As she talked about it, she got more excited about the prospect, but there was still a part of her who thought she was running away. That part of her felt guilty because she didn't intend to tell Tom or anyone else what she was up to.

Tom anxiously waited for Kathy to text him back about the doctor visit. By now, Tom was well-acquainted with the view of London from his room. He stared at the cityscape for hours and hours after their business meetings ended. Gene wanted to help his friend, but he knew he couldn't until Tom asked for it. He quietly prayed for opportunities to share. He did notice the level of Scotch in the bottle didn't seem to be dropping as rapidly. He saw that as a sign. Although Gene had known him for 20 years, there many guarded places when it came to Tom Kinsey.

"Kathy said there were pieces of glass in Lisa's hand," said Tom.

"How did she do that?"

"I think she threw the vase of roses I sent her against the wall, and when she tried to clean it up, she cut herself while talking to me. I guess my gift didn't go over too well."

Tom paused.

"Kathy's text said she didn't see a large crystal vase, but several smaller vases with flowers in them. She recognized the vases as ones Lisa already had," Tom continued.

"Do you blame her?"

Tom looked at the floor and shook his head.

"No, I guess I can't blame her."

"Put yourself in her position."

"Gene, have you ever had feelings for someone else since you married Kathy?"

Gene was surprised at the question but had a ready answer.

"Do you remember my assistant about three years ago?"

"I think so. Redhead, petite, liked to color-code all your files?"

Gene nodded.

"Really?" Tom seemed surprised. "I had no idea."

"No one did. She was going through a difficult divorce, and she began to confide in me details she shouldn't have. I took her to lunch several times, and then, I realized she was developing an attraction to me because I listened to her. And the feeling was mutual. She was a beautiful and intelligent woman. I could see it was heading in a direction I didn't want it to go. It wasn't long after that that I called a mutual friend of yours and mine, and I helped her find another job. It was actually a better job. I got one last phone call. It was a big thank you, not only for finding her another job, but for sparing both of us a mess. Then, I saw her and her new husband about a year later while I was at lunch with Kathy. She introduced me to him, and they seemed very happy."

Tom nodded.

"And during that time, I tried to invest more into my relationship with Kathy. I realized that if I was looking elsewhere, then there was something wrong with me; there was something wrong with us. I promised 'til death do us part.' And I meant it."

Gene took a deep breath.

"And that's also when Kathy and I really started going deeper into our spiritual journey together."

Tom rolled his eyes and started to stand up.

"You asked so sit down."

Tom raised his eyebrows at Gene and complied.

"We began to pray together. We began to attend a couples' Bible study, and things changed for us. We even went to some marriage counseling. I learned so much during that time. I can truthfully say I love her more today than I did the day I married her."

Tom took in what Gene was saying, but he didn't know how to respond. Gene moved his chair closer to Tom so he could look directly into his eyes.

"You need to sleep. We need to finish up this business deal as quickly as possible, and you need to get home to your wife. You can't throw away everything the two of you have. You've been together too long, and I know you love each other. She's wounded, and you have got to be part of the healing process."

Tom nodded.

"I'm going to get some sleep. Go to bed," said Gene.

8

Lisa tried to stay below Kathy's radar over the next week as she made preparations for her trip to Africa. One of those preparations included the meeting the Rev. Davis had invited her to attend. She arrived at the church fellowship hall as the meeting was getting started, and she tried to slide in the back unnoticed. There were about 30 people in the room filled with steel folding chairs. The Rev. Davis opened in prayer, and then, he made an announcement.

"I need to introduce someone to you," he said.

Lisa hated being the center of attention. Anytime she was called out it made her uncomfortable.

"Mrs. Kinsey, would you come down."

So much for anonymity, she thought, as she walked to stand next to the pastor.

"This is Lisa Kinsey; she's the reporter who will be traveling with us. In journalistic lingo, I believe they call them 'embedded' reporters. She will be taking a lot of photographs and interviewing people. She will also be documenting our progress on the website. Do you have anything you want to say?"

"Hi. I'm sure I'll meet all of you soon enough."

She smiled and returned to her seat.

"The purpose of tonight is to fill in the final details of the trips. Everyone here has the dates for their shift. Our project manager is in Kenya and has a list of the villages where we will be going to drill wells. The orphanage plans are also ready. It will be built near Nairobi but not in the city itself."

Rev. Davis moved to the back of the room where a laptop had been set up; he had a computer presentation about the different villages. For the next 20 minutes, he showed photographs of dry river beds and families who traveled long distances in search of water.

"We learned last week from one of the pastors in a village that one of the women there had been attacked and killed by a crocodile. She was in search of water and ended up too close to its habitat."

Lisa heard a collective gasp as she tried to comprehend the desperate situation these people faced daily. It made her own problems seem insignificant. She realized she was so blessed not to have to strive to find clean water. When she saw the faces of the people, her heart broke. As she sat through the meeting, she knew she was making the right decision. She knew she'd be making a difference in the lives of so many by simply reporting what was taking place.

As Rev. Davis finished his presentation, Lisa realized she probably looked like a mess. Tears streaked her face. Several members of the group then took the stage to tell about why they were making the trip. She heard about the sacrifices they were making. Many of them had worked hard to raise money to pay for their airfare and other expenses, but there was such a joy in their faces as they talked. They shared their love for God and how their love for Him was leading them to help people they'd never seen.

"People have criticized me for wanting to go to Africa. They say I should help people here," said one of the men. "I get that. I really do, but over there, they truly have nothing. There are charities and social programs here that exist to help people. I support those places too. I work at the food bank and have volunteered at the soup kitchen, but over there, they don't have options. I've met these precious people before, and I want to help them in some small way because I'm so blessed."

Many of them had stories like that.

"I've been on several foreign missions," said one woman. "I've been to Haiti, and I've been to Nicaragua. People here don't know poverty like they do over there. I go because it makes me so much more thankful for what I have. I've taken my kids too. They are much more appreciative now. They don't always want the biggest and the newest with the top brand."

Lisa remembered the trips she took as a teenager. She also realized that the empty feeling in her heart wasn't because Tom was unfaithful or Brittany was away at college or that she didn't have her regular job. She realized she missed the relationship she had with God. She'd tried to fill the empty place with so many other things, and while many of them were good things, they could never bring the fulfillment He could.

She stayed after they'd concluded to meet the people she'd been going on the trip with. As she finished talking to one of the women, she noticed the Rev. Davis sitting on a chair playing with his keys.

"You wanted to leave a while ago, didn't you?" she asked. "I'm sorry. Sometimes, I can talk a lot."

"No, no. It's not a problem at all. Actually, I wanted to ask you a few questions."

"Okay."

"What's going on with your husband?"

Lisa wasn't expecting that question. Her face fell, and she sat back down.

"Are you always this direct?" she asked.

He laughed.

"Sorry. I can be. I'm concerned. I don't know you, but you've seemed on the verge of tears from the moment I met you. And I don't think those tears are for children in Africa."

Something about his direct question hit Lisa. She wasn't sure if she'd be able to hold in her emotion. She took a deep breath.

"We are supposed to celebrate our 25th wedding anniversary in December. We've known each for 27 years. We've had a great life together until a few months ago. Our son graduated from college and moved away. Our daughter started college, and my husband pulled away. I lost my job. Then, my husband, Tom, admitted to having an affair. Now, he's in London trying to patch up a business deal this affair almost blew. The thing is that she lives in London. He took his friend, Gene, with him. Gene's a good guy. He also works for Tom. I guess Tom thinks Gene can babysit him or something."

Lisa stopped. She couldn't believe she'd told this stranger her whole life story, but she liked the Rev. Davis. She was able to drop her guard around him; however, the words spilled out of her with a cold anger. She didn't like her tone at all.

"So how do you feel about all of this?"

"Hurt, betrayed, worthless. How does anyone feel? I've gone from numb to being angry to wanting to hurt my husband to wanting to curl up in a ball and die all in the span of a few days," she said trying to hold back the tears. "And angry. I've felt really angry."

"Crying is okay," he said as he handed her some tissue. "How long has he been gone?"

"In a couple of days, it will be two weeks. All of this Africa stuff happened right after he left."

"And you haven't told him?"

"No."

"You don't think you should tell him?"

"I probably should, but I'm not going to. I don't know how long he's going to be in London. This is something I have to do now. You see, when I was a teenager, I went on several mission trips. I was even going to school to go into ministry, but when I met Tom, I shelved all of that for him. This time, I'm not. I don't know what part I will play, but I have to do this," she said.

The Rev. Davis nodded. He could see her determination.

"I believe you are right, and the way things turn out just might surprise you."

"I hope it's a good surprise."

"If I was a betting man, I'd say it was a sure thing that it will be a very good surprise."

The next morning Mr. Devereux's messenger arrived at her house with a large brown envelope. Inside it was a bigger check than she'd seen made out to her in a long time. She could tell he was mainly interested in polishing his son's reputation. Rumor had it the younger Devereux was being groomed for the U.S. Senate, and all of the nastiness of youth needed to be erased from memory. Photos of him holding starving children and building orphanages would be a great image builder. Plus, she was sure there'd be meetings with some important people as well. He'd already been seen doing some things locally, but he needed some foreign policy experience as well, she surmised. But regardless of the younger Devereux's intent, she knew others in the group had their hearts in the right places.

Also included in her package was a phone for her to use while in Africa and information on her flights. It would take at least 16 hours to get there, but the first flight left two days earlier than she thought. She still hadn't said anything to Brittany. She didn't know what to say, and her Thanksgiving break would begin soon.

As she pondered, she received a text from Brittany.

"Hey, Mom. My roommate's family is going skiing over Thanksgiving and asked me to come."

"That's exciting. Have fun."

Instead of responding with a text, Brittany called her mother.

"Mom, is everything okay?" Brittany asked.

"Of course, it is," Lisa tried to fake it in her voice.

"You are going to let me go?" she squealed with excitement.

"Sure. Just don't break any bones."

"She said 'yes,'" Brittany screamed to her friend in her mother's ear.

"Have a good time," Lisa said as the phone went dead. "I love you, too."

With that taken care of, the only problem left was Kathy. She was well-meaning, but Lisa felt like she was being spied on. She wasn't going to tell Kathy where she was going because she'd tell Tom. If Tom really wanted her, he'd have to find her. She wasn't going to make it easy on him. Their phone conversations over the past few days had become strained. Lisa was trying to sort out her anger, but all she did was pour it on him. She didn't want to act that way either. It wasn't helping matters. In his last conversation, he said he would probably be home the week after Thanksgiving.

Early on the day her flight was scheduled to leave, she met with Jessie Rose. She needed to give the paper her other cell phone number in case they had questions. She also had an envelope.

"Jessie, my kids have plans for Thanksgiving, and they don't know Tom is in London for reasons other than business. I'm not telling him where I'm going. If he should come to you and ask you questions, only give him this and nothing more. You and the people associated with this project are the only ones who know I'm leaving. If anyone cares enough, they'll track me down, and I haven't made it extremely difficult."

"Why would he come to me?"

"If he wants me back, he will," she said. "And I'm counting on him coming to you."

"I hope your faith isn't misplaced."

"Me too, and thanks for not saying 'I told you so,'" Lisa said as she hugged Jessie.

"I told you I wouldn't do that because I've always cared about you, and that's something no one wants to hear."

"True, but you could have said it. You were right. It only took 27 years, but you were right."

Her flight left late in the evening, but there was a two hour drive to the airport. She was riding with some of the other members of the group. Ironically, her flight had a layover in London before heading to Nairobi. She was ready to head to Rev. Davis' church when Kathy stopped by.

Lisa looked at her watch.

"Right on time," she said.

Kathy stared at the suitcases.

"Are you going somewhere?"

"Possibly."

"Where are you going?"

"I'm not telling you because you will run back and tell my secrets. If Tom Kinsey asks you where I am, he will be able to find a key to the puzzle here, but please, don't call him as soon as I leave."

"That's a little cryptic, don't you think?"

"Maybe, but it should be easy enough for him to figure out, and if he doesn't, well maybe things are headed in just the direction they need to be. Now, Kathy, if you will excuse me, I have an appointment."

She stood with the door open until Kathy walked out the kitchen door. Kathy glanced at Lisa with a confused look as she got into her car. Lisa followed and as she pulled of the driveway, her phone vibrated alerting an incoming text, but she wouldn't get it. She'd purposely left her phone on their bed on top of an envelope containing his first key to the puzzle.

The text was from Tom.

"Angel, I miss you. I'll be home for Thanksgiving."

Tom and Gene had gone out to celebrate their signing all the necessary contracts. It had been a long few weeks as Tom plunged head first into the business at hand and moved his attention away from Christine. He'd seen her a couple of times in the office, but her bosses agreed to his request to deal with different people on the project.

Tom was puzzled there was no return text from Lisa. As he stared at his phone, he heard familiar voice.

"I hear congratulations are in order for you, Tommy, and that you are leaving me for good," said Christine, who was holding a drink in her hand. It was obvious that she'd already had several.

Tom stood.

"Are you okay?"

"Just fine, all things considered. I'm hurt that you haven't come to see me any since you've been here."

"I'm sorry about that, but I couldn't continue this deal with you."

"Ah, but I thought our time together was only sealing the deal. That's usually the way it works. I scratch your back, and you scratch mine," Christine stumbled, and Tom stood to steady her.

"Why don't we get you a cab, Ms. Pennington?" Gene suggested.

"I'm not ready to go home yet. The night is young, and I feel like celebrating," she said as she pressed against Tom. She touched the side of his face. "I like the way we celebrate, Tommy. Don't you?"

Gene cleared his throat, and Tom pushed her away slowly in an effort not to cause a scene.

"Christine, you're drunk, and Gene and I are going to make sure you get home safely," Tom stressed Gene's name, but Christine didn't pay attention.

"You are coming to my house, Tommy. That's what I wanted all along," she smiled.

Tom looked at Gene.

"I guess it's going to be another room service night," he said indicating for Gene to pay the bill for the meal they weren't going to get to eat.

They didn't have to wait long for the cab, and Christine couldn't keep her hands off Tom in the cab.

"Christine, give the man your address," he instructed.

She did. He kept removing her hands from him, but she quickly placed them back. She wasn't shy about her movements either. Fortunately, the ride wasn't far from where they'd been.

Gene had stayed in the cab as Tom helped Christine into her apartment. When they walked in, she began kissing him passionately. He pushed her away.

"Christine, I can't do this," he said.

"That was what you said last time, but we know how that turned out," she said as she moved back toward him.

"I was wrong. I love my wife. I love Lisa," he said as he moved backward to the door of her flat.

Gene stepped into the room, and he placed himself between Christine and Tom.

"Goodbye, Ms. Pennington," Gene said.

The cab was still waiting for them as they rushed down the stairs. Tom's hands were shaking. The cab ride to their hotel was quiet. Tom stared out the window.

As soon as they entered the hotel room, Gene asked Tom a question.

"If I hadn't been there to intervene, what would have happened?"

"I'm not sure," he said. "I hope that I would have left, but I still don't trust myself."

"Well at least you're honest."

"I'm glad you were there. In fact, I've been glad you were here the whole time," Tom said. "I realized why I was attracted to Christine and why I let my guard down before. It went back to when I was a little boy, and the helpless feeling I had of not being able to protect my mother. When Courtney, the teenager in the accident, died, I was helpless again. I realized somewhere along the way, I thought I wasn't needed any more by my own children, by my wife. I know Lisa was having problems with Brittany and Spencer being gone, but at least, she told me about it. I thought it didn't bother me. I had to be 'the man,' like my father said. I couldn't show weakness. I had to be the strong one. My little girl is grown. I'm not the invincible Daddy. She's hardly called or texted since she went off to school."

Tom sat in front of his familiar window. He paused for several minutes. Gene let him talk. This was what needed to happen.

"Lisa was trying to reach out to me, but I saw this young, attractive woman who stroked my ego. I ignored the one person who matters the most to me."

"I've been trying to tell you this for several days now," he said.

"You know me, Gene, I'm stubborn. I still have to learn lessons the hard way sometimes," he said. "And I've taken to heart what you've said. I brought you along on this trip for two reasons. The first is that you are a man of your word. You have integrity, and that's important to me. The second is you've been a rock of a friend, and I appreciate it more than you know. I've thought about many high points and some low ones we've gone through together. You've always been steady."

"Tom, I admire you too."

"Let me finish because this is getting ready to be difficult," he smiled. Gene hadn't seen that smile since they'd arrived.

"I remember the almost relationship you had. I didn't realize it until you told me what happened, but I saw a change in you after she left. It was a good change. You didn't stress out as much. Your customer skills became much better. You had a little more patience with people. And you admitted you didn't know everything that you were wrong sometimes."

Gene didn't answer.

"I've been trying to do all of this on my own. I've been trying to not become like my father on my own, and the harder I try, the worse it gets. I can't do it."

Tom looked straight at him. He seemed embarrassed.

"I want what you have," Tom said.

Gene wasn't able to hide his surprise.

"That's great, Tom," he said. "Let's pray."

As Tom prayed with Gene, Lisa was praying with the group headed to Africa. The Rev. Davis led them all in a prayer asking for protection on the journey as well as favor on their mission.

Lisa's brain kept telling her she was crazy, but there was something in her heart telling her she was making the right decision. She wanted to believe Tom loved her as he said. If he came after her as she hoped, she'd know he loved her and would be able to put the past behind her, behind them.

Lisa was the outsider in this group even though the people were kind to her. She wasn't going to do what they were. She would be as she always was - the fly on the wall, the observer. The ride to the airport was uneventful. They arrived in plenty of time for their check-in and flight. And on the plane, she was separated from them once again. It gave her time to think.

She tried to think about some of the good times. Tom liked puzzles and trying to figure things out. He also liked creating puzzles for her. The Christmas after he'd sold his first house he sent her on a quest for her present. He gave her an envelope with the first clue. The clues were related to dates they'd gone on and special things they'd done together. Some of the clues made her misty-eyed because she hadn't realized the details he'd remembered. He knew what she wore on their first date and where they went. Each time she solved a clue, she found another envelope until she went into the outdoor storage shed to find a very large box. He followed her every step of the way, taking photographs. He laughed with her, and when she cried, he smiled softly, knowing that he'd touched her heart. He brought the big box into the house. Inside each box was a smaller wrapped box until finally she came to a velvet box with ruby and diamond cocktail ring inside. She loved rubies. They were her birthstone. She glanced down at her right hand and stared at the ring he'd given her. It remained one of the most precious gifts he'd given.

He had always been such an amazing husband. What had happened? Where did things go wrong? Was there anything she could have done? They rarely fought, and she'd uttered more harsh words since he'd left than she could ever recall saying to him in their entire marriage. She didn't like what this was doing to her. Lashing out and having outbursts such as throwing the vase of roses was so unlike her. It didn't hurt him any, but she could attest to it hurting her. She still had a painful reminder in her left hand. Maybe, he did want things to be different

"Please God, let him come after me – and soon," she prayed under her breath.

"We will be landing at London Heathrow Airport in about 15 minutes," the pilot came over the intercom.

In London, Tom and Gene were preparing their trip home.

"I still haven't heard from Lisa," said Tom as they took a taxi

71

to Heathrow.

"Tom, she's probably asleep. After all, they are five hours be-hind us. That means it's 1 a.m. there," he said looking at his watch.

"You are right. I'll be able to see her soon enough," he said. "I can't wait to get home. I feel like I don't have a care in the world."

Gene smiled.

"I know what you mean," he said.

The line for security seemed to take forever, and although the two men had thought they'd arrived in plenty of time to make their flight, they were scurrying to the gate only to find boarding had al-ready begun. As they waited in line, Tom glanced around the airport. He shook his head. He saw a woman who looked like Lisa several gates over. He must have been more ready to return home than he thought. The line began to move, and Gene nudged Tom.

"What's the matter?"

"Nothing. I guess I'm really ready to be home. There's a woman at that far gate who looks like Lisa from here," he smiled, and they got on the plane.

Tom's eyes weren't playing tricks on him. It was Lisa he saw in the distance. She was thinking about him too. She wondered where in London he was staying. She wanted to see him, but he needed to go home first.

9

The group arrived in Kenya at nightfall. Exhausted from the long trip, most of them were ready to go to bed so they could be refreshed to start the new day. Many of them only had a week on the ground, and there was much work to be accomplished. Plans had changed several times. Now the plan was to stay from the day before Thanksgiving until after the start of the New Year with different team members coming in and out over that time. The hope was to dig several wells and build an orphanage in that time. The group had linked with other groups already in place in Africa to finish their task.

Lisa's flights were open to go home around Christmas and return a few days later. She wasn't sure exactly what she was doing. At this point, it depended on Tom.

Mr. Devereux had rented a place for them to stay in Nairobi. It was Americanized and had all of the trappings of home. Compared to the places they would be headed, it was the epitome of luxury. They could travel to the outlying villages via a van he had rented for them. Traveling to some of the villages would require overnight stays. Lisa wasn't really looking forward to those, but she'd do what was necessary. The early legs of the journey were close by. She would have some time to get acclimated before having to stay in the villages overnight.

Lisa knew Mr. Devereux was fronting a lot of money for this project, but he was worth so much she was sure he wouldn't miss it.

Besides, he was working on polishing his son's image for a campaign announcement that would happen within the next few years, and the cost didn't matter.

Rev. Davis called everyone together for a brief meeting.

"Set your watches seven hours ahead, and we will be leaving in the morning around 3 to go to our first village, which is about four hours away. While they are drilling the well, there are support ministries for us. We will be giving out food and shoes that the churches have sent over. Also, we will be there to show them the love of Jesus."

Lisa hoped her body clock would adjust to the time change as she dragged herself to her room, which had two twin beds. She had a roommate who was taking a semester off from college to be part of the trip.

Tom and Gene, too, had had a long flight plus a layover in New York City. During the layover, an early winter storm came through, causing many delays and flight cancellations. This led to problems with their cell phone service, and they couldn't call out or send messages. They would be arriving late at the airport two hours from home; they had left a car at the airport in long-term parking, and they planned to surprise their wives with their arrival.

Gene dropped Tom off at his house around 5 a.m. Thanksgiving Day. He went in the kitchen rather than the garage so he didn't notice Lisa's vehicle was missing.

Tom rushed into their bedroom in hopes of snuggling next to his wife, but he found the lamp illuminated on the bedside table, and an envelope marked "Clue 1" lying in the middle of the bed. Lisa had strategically set her cell phone on top of the envelope with the clue and her volume of Shakespeare.

"So we are going to be dramatic, are we?" Tom said out loud.

He picked up the cell phone. Its battery was dead. Calling her to find out where she was had been eliminated from the picture.

"Dear Tom, you've always like puzzles and adventure so I have one for you if you dare," she wrote.   "Return to the day when our paths did first meet and talk to the lady whose name by any other would still smell as sweet."

Tom smiled. Instantly he knew what was going on. She'd mentioned that Christmas scavenger hunt on more than one occasion. It meant a lot to her. He'd asked her once why, and she told him it was all of the thought and time that went into it. It made her feel special. Also, all of the details he remembered made her know how much she was loved. She was counting on him remembering those small details.

"That's my girl," he said aloud. "I do love you."

He understood her clues. He knew Lisa was referring to the passage in Shakespeare's Romeo and Juliet about a rose, and he remembered their first meeting when she interviewed him for the college newspaper about the food drive. She showed up that day in 1986 wearing jeans, a white blouse and a black blazer with leopard print lapels and thick shoulder pads. He was sure she'd used an entire can of hairspray to get her hair that big and her bangs perfect.

"I'm looking for Tom Kinsey," she said as she approached his table.

"You have found him," he said and smiled.

She reached out to shake his hand.

"Lisa Miller with the University Press, we spoke on the phone about the drive," she said in her most businesslike tone.

She later would tell him she fell for him the instant he smiled and said she'd found him. Her heart had decided at that moment she'd found the one she'd spend the rest of her life with.

The interview went smoothly as Tom showed her the boxes and filled with food and told her college students could get a coupon for a free hamburger at one of the local businesses if they dropped off a canned good. The club Tom was a part of required its members to perform community service events throughout the semester.

Lisa snapped a few photos to go along with the story. Her deadline was fast approaching, and since she was new to the school paper, she was nervous about finishing the story on time. She had to rush her film to the lab across campus, where the photography students would process it for the paper. In her haste and nervousness, she dropped her notebook, and they bashed heads as both of them bent to pick it up. Lisa ended up falling backwards and sitting on the floor looking up at him. Tom laughed at the incident, but Lisa looked horrified. The natural color drained from beneath the blush-stained cheeks. He helped her up, and she darted for the open door, hoping no one else saw her fall.

Tom had to wait for the food drive to end to locate Lisa. He bought a bouquet of flowers and bottle of aspirin which he attached to a straw with ribbon and slid into the center of the bouquet. When he arrived at the college newspaper office, the first person he encountered was Jessie Rose. She never approved of Tom. She thought Lisa was naïve and that he would take advantage of her. When she saw him enter the office with the flowers, she tried to block him.

"What are you doing here, Mr. Kinsey?"

"I have a delivery."

"You can't bribe a journalist."

He smiled.

"I'm not trying to bribe anyone."

Lisa saw him enter and tried to hide behind a partition. When she peeked out, he saw her and headed straight for her. There was nowhere to run.

"I've been told I'm very hard-headed. I hope I didn't do any permanent damage," he said as he handed her the bouquet. He grabbed her hand and kissed it. Then, he nodded and headed out of the office. As he approached Jessie, he grandly bowed to her and motioned as though he was tipping an invisible hat. He grinned as he walked out of the door.

Lisa was mesmerized as he left the office. She stared into the mixed bouquet of roses and carnations. No one had given her flowers before. Jessie tried to snap her out of her daydream.

"He is trouble, Lisa," said Jessie. "Mark my words – trouble."

Lisa giggled as she saw the bottle of aspirin tucked inside the bouquet.

"Jessie, you could be right, but he is beautiful. And he has a great sense of humor."

Tom thought about that day. He knew the story of how Jessie Rose had inspired Lisa to go into journalism, but he also knew Jessie's opinion of him.

"You really are angry with me, aren't you, Lisa," Tom voiced his thoughts out loud as he sat on their bed. "Jessie still hates me. She probably hates me even more now. And I have to call her on one of the few holidays the newspaper gives most of its employees. I hope she'll be working Black Friday and not out shopping."

He went to the computer and tried to find some type of alternate phone number for Jessie, but he could only locate her work number. He looked around the desk to see if Lisa had written down a cell number or given him another clue. That would be too easy. No, he was going to have to work for this.

He dialed her number. He could at least leave a voicemail.

"Hi. This is Jessie Rose, arts and entertainment reporter. I will be out of the office Thanksgiving Day, but I will be in the office and avoiding the mall on Black Friday."

"Jessie Rose, this is Tom Kinsey. Please call me as soon as you get this message."

Just then, Tom's phone rang. It was Gene.

"Gene, go to bed."

"Tom, they are preparing for an Army at my house. The chefs are already in full swing even at this time of day. There are already pies in the oven. Come and eat with us today. I understand you are going to be alone."

"The house is empty."

"I'll see you at noon."

"Gene, I would rather be alone."

"Not an option according to Kathy."

"Fine," said Tom as he hung up the phone.

He went into his office and pulled the bottle of Scotch out of his desk. He placed the bottle in front of him and stared at it for a few minutes.

"God, I don't know how to pray without Gene here. I don't want this bottle to rule my life. Please help me. Help me get these thoughts out of my head," he prayed.

He took the bottle into the kitchen and cried as he poured its contents down the drain.

10

Thanksgiving in Africa was like any other day of the year. On this particular day, Lisa couldn't imagine feasting and football games. They were spending it in a remote village, drilling the first well. At home, Thanksgiving did have a bit of excitement to it. There was the hustle and bustle of the meal, and family gathered. Then, after the meal, Lisa and the kids would begin decorating for Christmas while the games played in the background. The excitement she felt on this Thanksgiving was different. They were going to take water to people who had none. She could tell the pastor and the team members who were giving up time with family and friends were more excited about their mission than a holiday.

"We wanted to come to the area where the situation was the most desperate," Rev. Davis explained to the group. "And we've found it. There's a small church outreach here. An African pastor travels through this area regularly. He's part of the bigger team on the ground. Also, we've done geographic surveys. We will probably have to drill deep to find water here. The ground is so hard from years of no water, and there are areas of rock we will have to drill through as well."

The people of the village were curious about the massive truck and the support vehicles the team brought with them. They'd never seen anything like it. Their reality was so different from Lisa's. They didn't have televisions with 24-hour news, weather and entertainment. They stared at the foreigners from afar at first.

Lisa met the African pastor and the interpreter. In her early 50s, the interpreter spoke several languages and was a nurse.

"I'm so happy you all have come," she said. "This is a miracle for them."

"We are so happy to have you with us. You don't know what this means for us," said the Rev. Davis.

Lisa found herself doing some videography as well. She brought her personal camcorder along and panned the area. People needed to see the view they were seeing. There was a small "church" building in the village. It was a simple structure with a tin roof and a couple of walls. The floor was the reddish dirt that covered the area. The landscape had sparse trees and dried brush. The people in the village lived in small circular huts made of sticks and thatched roofs.

There was one doctor and a nurse on the support team. They had some limited medical supplies, and they did what they could. The interpreter told Lisa they could do so much more if only there were more people like the ones helping them now.

"This area is ravaged by diseases such as HIV. The mothers infect the little ones," she said. "Then, the mothers die. Because of malnutrition and the drought, it's not long before the little ones die too."

Some of the hardest stories Lisa had ever worked on in her years of journalism were ones including sick children. She could tug on people's heartstrings when she wrote on the struggles of children. Usually, it was tied to a non-profit or some type of organization raising money for sick kids. She hoped those stories would help people want to reach deep into their pockets to help if they were able. Money couldn't solve all the world's ills, but it definitely helped.

She knew her stories from here would help as well.

The day of drilling did not go well. Those manning the truck encountered difficulty after difficulty, and one of the parts on the drill broke. They had back-up parts, but it would take some time to repair the drill. Lisa watched and snapped photos as the Rev. Davis gathered team members in a circle to pray.

"Lord, please give us wisdom on where to drill. We want to bring water to these people. You've brought us this far, and we thank You. Back home, our families and friends are celebrating Thanksgiving. We are thankful as well. We want to thank You for leading us here and thank You for success, Amen." he said.

It would be getting dark soon. After consulting with the drill team foreman, they decided to call it a very long day. She could tell the members of the group were discouraged; even Rev. Davis, who always had a huge smile, looked haggard. The ride to the village had taken several hours, and it would be a long drive back for the support team. The drilling team would remain in the village overnight. It would probably take most of the next day to repair the broken part. The support team had another village to go to in the morning. The pastor had let people know about the medical clinic.

Dusty and dirty from a long day, team members took quick showers before going to bed. Lisa almost felt guilty watching the water swirl down the drain when that water was worth more than gold and diamonds a few hours away.

She was tired, but she couldn't sleep. The thoughts she'd suppressed on the day were now coming to the surface. She thought about Tom, and she wondered where he might be. Did he make it home by Thanksgiving? He wasn't supposed to be home yet, but he'd sounded hopeful he'd finish early. Would he figure out the first clue? It was easy, but they did get harder. And there was this part of her that felt guilty doing something so totally out of her character. She couldn't believe she'd flown across the globe without telling anyone.

Lisa decided she couldn't stay in the bed any longer. She got dressed and walked out into the living room, where she found the Rev. Davis with an open Bible in his lap and his eyes closed. She tried to walk quietly past him. There was a dining room she could go into to find a quiet spot to think.

"You don't have to tiptoe. I'm not asleep. Just trying to get guidance. We have to get water into that village," he said in a desperate tone.

"I understand. I want to see their faces when the water begins to flow out of the well," she said.

"It will be a sight to see. Why aren't you asleep?"

"In the past few weeks, I haven't known what sleep is. Sometimes, I can't get my mind to shut off," she said. "You know, this is not like any Thanksgiving I've ever celebrated in my life. No turkey, no feasting, no football games, but today, after seeing those faces and where they live, I am more thankful today than I've ever been."

"I understand that. Let me ask you another question. What did you give to my secretary for safe keeping?"

Lisa was surprised.

"She told you about that?"

He nodded.

"She tells me everything I need to know," he said and grinned. "There are some things she holds back though."

"I gave her a puzzle piece."

He raised an eyebrow.

"It's complicated," she said.

"A game?"

"Not really. It's actually a matter of life and death where my marriage is concerned."

He still looked confused.

"You'd have to know my husband. He likes challenges, the thrill of the hunt, but with a quirky, even romantic twist. So, I'm giving him one. No one knows where I am except for two people at the newspaper, Mr. Devereux and your secretary. My kids weren't going to make it home for Thanksgiving so I didn't bother to tell them," she said. "I left my personal cell phone at home with the first clue. If my husband really wants me back, he'll accept my challenge and show up here."

"Is this wise?"

"I don't know, but it's something I have to try. I haven't been myself lately. This is so not Lisa Kinsey to fly across the world with a group of people she doesn't even know. I thought about all of this for a long time before mapping out Tom's clues. Maybe he went after that other woman because he felt the same emptiness I've felt. I wasn't unhappy with Tom, but I knew there was something more. If he's not here in 10 days or less, I guess I'll have my answer. All I know is that being here I'm finally starting to feel alive again. I have a purpose once more. As far as Tom, it's out of my hands now. He has to make the next move. I don't know what else to do, but I do know I'm not going to stop living."

She shrugged her shoulders and started to head back to her room.

"Good night, Rev," she said and paused. "You know, I still have problems calling you that because you just don't look like a pastor. I guess you've never heard that one before."

"Nope, never," he said and grinned. "Call me Matt. I don't know why you've been calling me Rev. Davis all this time anyway. I thought you heard everyone call me 'Matt.'"

She nodded.

"Goodnight, Matt, and tomorrow will be a much better day. I'm almost positive of it," she said and mustered the biggest smile she could.

"I like your positive emotion, and I'll second it," he said and laughed. "Hey, in my profession, we call that 'faith.'"

Lisa smiled at him and nodded. Her thoughts ran back to the day he asked her if she was a woman of faith.

"Well, maybe there's a little faith left after all," she said.

"I think there's a lot of faith left. Good night," he said.

Tom could say some of the same things about his Thanksgiving that Lisa did. It was definitely not like any he'd had, but while Lisa was grateful for the things she had, Tom was kicking himself for the things and people he was without.

He wasn't going to accept Kathy and Gene's invitation for Thanksgiving dinner, but both of them called several times. Gene even threatened to drive to his house to pick him up, but he knew he'd be at their mercy on a return home. At least if he drove, he could leave when he wanted. He told them he didn't think he'd be good company, but they wouldn't listen.

"Tom, you look awful," said Kathy as he arrived at their home.

"Thanks. It's lovely to see you as well," he said as he gave her a quick hug.

"Come in. I think you know everyone here."

Tom scanned the room. Gene and Kathy's two teenagers plus Gene's and Kathy's parents were there. Fortunately, no one else from the office was there. Kathy didn't like for people to be alone on holidays, and she often made room for single people who for some reason didn't have anyone else to spend them with. Her gift was hospitality, and she could make new people feel at ease in the most awkward situations.

"We will eat in about 30 minutes. Can I get you something, Tom?" she asked.

"No, actually, I was wondering if I could have a word with you."

"Of course, but I don't have any other information on Lisa."

Kathy read his mind as headed into the kitchen. She had cooked enough food to feed three times the number of people that had gathered for the celebration. Everything had finished cooking, but she was putting the finishing touches on the presentation. She liked for the food to look as good as it tasted. Gene joined them in the kitchen. Kathy wanted the turkey cut and placed on a platter rather than the whole bird put on the table. She didn't like the carcass left there during the meal.

"Kathy, please tell me what's been going on with Lisa since I left," he asked.

"I think I've told you everything. She's lost weight over the past several weeks. Not that she needs to, but I could tell that. Her clothes hung off her body. She doesn't eat, and she's been withdrawn. She doesn't sleep either. She has dark circles under her eyes that she tries to hide with concealer. I visited her on several occasions including the night she cut her hand. Last time I checked that was healing. There was no real damage except for the pieces of crystal he had to remove from her hand."

"Tell me about the last time you saw her."

"It was on Monday. I went over to say 'hello' and she was headed somewhere with two big suitcases and a couple of small ones."

"And she didn't say where?"

"No, Tom. She didn't want me to know because she thought I'd tell you. I guess she knew you'd be pumping me for information."

"What exactly did she say? Do you remember?"

"She didn't say much except 'if Tom Kinsey asks you where I am, he will be able to find a key to the puzzle here.' And that was an exact quote by the way. I committed it to memory in case you asked. When I told her I thought she was being cryptic, she said it should be easy for you to figure out, and that if you didn't, then she had the answers to the questions."

"Did she meet someone?"

Kathy was about to pour hot gravy into a bowl, but she put the pot down to look at him. She raised her head and narrowed her eyes into an icy glare.

"I do know that is an emphatic 'no.' I can't believe you would even suggest it, and if you didn't sign my husband's paychecks, I would punch you for her," she said. "I know Lisa loves you, and I know she's angry. I don't know where she's gone, but it's not to be with another man if that's what you are asking. She started going back to church. She's gone with me a couple of times. That's the only thing out of the ordinary I know."

Kathy went back to the task of filling the gravy boat.

"Would you put this on the table?" she asked as she handed it to him.

He quickly put it on the table, and when he returned, she asked him what the puzzle key was.

"It was a poem and the key to another clue. She's sending

me on a scavenger hunt. That's the reason she went away. I believe I'll find her at the end. She's the prize. I'm sure there's not another man involved. I wasn't thinking when I asked that question. It was a stupid thing to say."

"Is this some sort of sick game she's playing?" Kathy asked.

"No. It's not. I know what she's doing. My first clue had a bad poem and a memory," he smiled. "I think there will be several bad poems and memories attached until I find her. I guess it's her way of making me think about the good times we had and leading a path to her."

"Why couldn't she have just been here when you got home?"

"Now, that would be too easy, wouldn't it? Besides, she doesn't know I'm home. The last I'd told her was next week with an unlikely hope of being home for Thanksgiving. She knew she would be well into her destination before I got there. Lisa always believed you had to work at a relationship, and I haven't been doing my share of it lately," he said as he looked down at Kathy's tiled kitchen counters. "I'm back on the job today."

"So where will you find your next clue?"

"I have to call someone at the newspaper tomorrow."

"I'm starting to get worried about her," said Kathy.

"Gene, do you remember me telling you about the woman I saw at Heathrow?"

"Yes," Gene didn't look up from his turkey carving duties.

"What are you talking about?" asked Kathy.

"I swear I saw Lisa in Heathrow when we were leaving."

"What would she be doing in England?"

"I have no idea, but she was waiting at the gate so she's not in England. She was waiting for another plane," he said. "And that could take her anywhere."

Tom made the best of the day. He smiled and made small talk. Despite Gene and Kathy's protests, he helped clean up so he could make a swift departure. He wanted to get some rest because he had a feeling Black Friday was going to be a long day, and it wouldn't be from standing in shopping lines.

11

Newspaper reporters don't keep bankers' hours, and Jessie arrived at the office around 11 a.m. for a long day. Tom wasn't exactly sure of her hours so he arrived around 9:30 and waited in the newsroom lobby.

"Waiting for me?" Jessie spotted him as soon as she got off the elevator. She only paused for a second before heading to her mailbox and then to her desk. Tom followed. "I'm impressed. Maybe, Lisa's faith isn't misplaced after all. She never would listen to me."

"It's good to see you too, Jessie," he said.

She raised an eyebrow at him, and then, she opened a desk drawer, pulling out the envelope Lisa had given her.

"I believe this is why you are here?"

"Did she say anything else when she gave this to you?"

Jessie laughed.

"She said to only give you this and nothing else, and you can quote me on it."

"Thank you."

As he turned to leave, Jessie grabbed his arm and lowered her voice.

"Tom, make things right with her. She's always believed in you. She's always been a good woman and a good friend. She looked like she'd been through the ringer, and she deserves better than that."

"I know you've never liked me. I know I've made some terrible mistakes, but I want to make things right."

Jessie poked him in center of his chest and nodded.

"You'd better, and it's going to take more than flowers and aspirin this time."

"Yes, ma'am," Tom smiled and bowed dramatically as he left the room.

Despite his urge to tear open the envelope immediately, he waited until he got into his car. He looked at the white envelope. She'd written "Tom – Clue 2" in her frilliest cursive on the front of it with a pink marker

"All's fair in love, and the winner takes the prize. Go back home, and you'll see what you've wanted was always there before your eyes," read the note in the same frilly pink script.

"Okay, what does that mean, Lisa?" he said softly as he headed back to the house.

He tried to think on the way home what she could have meant. The first clue took him back to the beginning of their relationship and how they'd met. They'd read a lot of marriage books together over the years, and one of the things all of them said was to never let the spark go out and keep the reasons you fell in love in the first place alive. Was this clue another from the early days?

"All's fair in love," he said as he tried to pay attention the road and figure out the clue at the same time. "Not love and war. Isn't that the quote? She left off the war part. I guess we aren't in a war?"

Lisa and Tom had never been at war with each other. Sure, they had their share of arguments and disagreements, but they always managed to work things out. He wondered what he should look for when he got back home. As he wandered through the rooms, nothing seemed to stand out to him. He went into the living room and scanned their bookshelf. He searched the DVD titles and went through several photo albums.

"What exactly am I looking for Lisa?" he asked out loud.

He traveled into his office. Everything seemed to be in the same place where he'd left it the week before. He opened desk drawers and moved books. After a couple of hours, he began to get frustrated. He reread the clue several times.

"Fair, fair," he said. "All's fair in love. Is your clue in the bedroom, Lisa?"

He went into their bedroom and glanced around.

"Okay, it's something right before my eyes," he said.

He sat on the edge of the bed. What was right before his eyes? From his vantage point, he could see Lisa's dresser. There were a couple of framed photographs of them and their children, her jewelry box, a silk flower arrangement, and oh yes, that had it be it, an ugly, hot pink teddy bear, which she refused to part with. He picked it up and held it in his hands. Their first date was a trip to the fair. He'd asked her out a few days after taking her flowers. He remembered calling the school newspaper.

"Lisa, Trouble is on the phone asking for you," Jessie had answered the phone.

"What are you talking about?"

"Tom Kinsey."

Lisa felt her pulse quicken when she knew Tom was on the phone.

"Hi, this is Lisa," she picked up the phone in her most professional reporter voice.

"Hey, Tom Kinsey. I just wanted to thank you for the great story in the college paper today."

Jessie had moved closer to Lisa's desk.

"Trouble" she mouthed the words at Lisa while Lisa tried to shoo her away.

"You're welcome. I was glad to get the word out for you. I hope it will help your upcoming charity events be successful."

"I'm sure they will. Thanks for putting in some of the other things we are doing."

There was an awkward pause.

"Lisa, I was wondering if you would like to go out with me? The fair is in town this weekend."

"Well, I..." she started.

"You already have plans?"

"No, I..."

"Is Madame Editor telling you not to go with me?"

"Jessie? Yes, but..."

"Don't listen to her. I can pick you up Friday night," he said.

"Well."

"I'll be there at 6."

"Okay."

Lisa hung up the phone. She felt exhilarated and nervous all at the same time. She tried not to look Jessie in the eyes.

"I can't believe it," said Jessie. "You are going out with him."

Lisa nodded.

"He's a heartbreaker. Look at the eyes and that smile. Oh yes, and the teeth. Womanizers always have awesome teeth," said Jessie.

Lisa laughed. He did have an amazing smile.

"He has a great smile. Yes, he does have great teeth, but it's the smile Jessie. It's the smile. He's not the Big Bad Wolf, you know. Besides, how do you know about Tom?"

"Experience with other guys just like him."

"How do you know he's like other guys?"

"It's those hunches journalists and cops get," Jessie replied without a hint of humor in her voice. "Mark my words. He will hurt you one day and very badly. Remember the teeth. He is the Big Bad Wolf, Lisa, despite what you may believe. Those teeth will chew you up and spit you out."

Lisa's smile had disappeared. What if Jessie was right? He was gorgeous, and he had perfect pearly white teeth.

When Friday arrived, Tom promptly appeared at the door at 6 p.m. Lisa lived with her mother in a small apartment. Her mother wasn't exactly warm when he first came in. Lisa hadn't dated a lot of people. Working a couple of jobs plus going to school fulltime and writing for the school newspaper left her little opportunity for socializing.

Tom chatted with Lisa's mother while he awaited her appearance. She wasn't quite ready. She wanted to look perfect. Tom had a way of disarming people. They felt comfortable around him. Within a few minutes, Tom had won her mother over.

She wore a hot pink fluffy sweater with a long-sleeve white shirt underneath; the cuffs of her white shirt were folded back over the sweater, which she'd pushed to three-quarter length. Of course, the sweater had shoulder pads the size of mini-pillows. She wore stonewashed jeans and white sneakers. Her chestnut brown hair was perfectly curled and sprayed into place.

"You look stunning," he said.

She blushed.

"I promise not to keep her out too late, Mrs. Miller," he said to Lisa's mom.

It was a crisp fall night on the midway. Neon lights from the Ferris wheel and various rides flashed, and the sounds of the music from the rides clashed with the laughter of children and the screams from those suspended upside down in cars in mid-air.

"Are you hungry, my lady?" asked Tom.

Lisa glanced around.

"There are corn dogs and fries over there and cotton candy and funnel cakes over there," he pointed to the different vendors. "Oh and there are greasy onion rings down that way."

Lisa laughed.

"A corn dog is probably good," she said.

"A corn dog it is. What did the evil editor tell you about me?"

"She's not evil. I think she means well."

Lisa and Tom found a picnic table and sat down.

"Did she tell you I'd eat you for breakfast and spit you out before lunch?"

"She told me you had great teeth," Lisa laughed.

"Ah, all the better to devour you."

"That's exactly what she said," Lisa nodded.

Tom's smile faded.

"And what do you think?"

"I'm a journalist. I'm impartial, and I take in all the facts."

"I see so the verdict is still out on me."

"Yes. I want to make an informed decision not based on hearsay or teeth."

"Maybe you should be a lawyer or judge rather than a journalist."

"I like to write, and I don't want to be around criminals or those accused of breaking the law. I want to make a difference in people's lives."

Tom smiled.

"You do have great teeth," Lisa said it before she realized it. She blushed again.

"Thank you, and they are for devouring corn dogs not journalism majors," he said as he took a big bite out of his corn dog for added effect.

She smiled.

"So, what do you want to ride first? There's the Ferris wheel; there's a really cool rollercoaster. Do you like the ones that spin and the bottom falls out of the floor?"

"The bumper cars?" Lisa hesitated. "I can't ride those others. They make me sick."

Tom shook his head and laughed.

"And I thought you didn't want to come with me to the fair because of what Jessie said about my teeth."

"Nope. It had nothing to do with Jessie, and everything to do with not wanting to have, well let's just say, unpleasant memories of tonight. Why don't we just walk around?"

They walked through the midway, and Tom ignored most of the carnival barkers begging him to come and try his skill for a prize for "the little lady." They talked about how ugly the neon-colored stuffed animals that hung from the stalls were.

"Hey, I think that one matches your sweater," said Tom, pointing to the one at the baseball throw game. "I used to play baseball in high school. Come on. You should have a souvenir from tonight."

They walked over to the booth. Tom got three baseballs, and soon, Lisa had a hot pink teddy bear to match her sweater. When he handed her the bear, he noticed she had a few tears in her eyes.

"I'm not doing well on this evening at all," he said.

"No, you are wonderful. Stuffed animals always remind me of my dad. He died, but he always gave me stuffed animals in unnatural colors for Easter and Valentine's Day and other random days. When we moved, I had to get rid of a lot of them. I still have a couple, but you should have seen my room. I will always treasure this bear. Thank you," she said and hugged him.

He seemed surprised.

"I'm sorry. I didn't mean to" she started.

"No, it's perfect." In that moment, he knew she was the woman he wanted to spend the rest of his life with.

"Are you sure?"

"Yes, why?"

"You are looking at me strangely."

Tom's demeanor had changed. Instead the charming, seductive Don Juan that Jessie had made him out to be, he had a tender look in his eyes as his tone became serious.

"You have the face of an angel. I've never seen anyone so beautiful."

She blushed. She heard Jessie's voice in her head about not falling for his charm. It was too late. She had collapsed into those deep blue eyes.

"How about those bumper cars?" she asked trying to change the mood.

"You're on."

After the bumper cars, it was the carousel, and a lot of walking hand-in-hand and talking about their plans after college. Lisa dreamed of working for the local newspaper. She had an interview there the following week about a summer internship, and there was the possibility of working part time as well. Tom dreamed of owning a successful business.

"We had our dreams, didn't we, Angel? Looks like we made most of them come true. Didn't we, ugly bear? You've been in this room and heard lots of things," he stared at the bear. It had a tiny key on a chain around its neck. He removed it and held it so it dangled from the chain. "I had to work to get you so I guess I'm going to have to work to get you back. Challenge accepted."

12

Lisa was finding it difficult to stay in her role as reporter. She wanted to help the people and forget about documenting everything. They needed her hands. The day after the drilling frustration they traveled to a different village to give out shoes and food at an orphanage. They'd brought some shoes with them to give away, but they also sent money ahead to the pastors in Nairobi to purchase them. With tears streaming down her face, she watched through the lens as the children received their shoes. They looked at them as something precious. While people back home were clamoring for the best Black Friday deals, these children were having an early Christmas. She wondered if they even knew what Christmas was. They were so excited. Lisa thought about all of the shoes she had in her closet back home, and these children might not have ever had more than one pair of shoes at a time. The head of the orphanage said some of them had never had a brand new pair just ones handed down from child to child until they fell apart. She knew of some places near the cities where children would find plastic bottles and strap them to their feet. They needed to cover their feet because of the sand fleas or jiggers as they are called.

Lisa snapped photo after photo. She was glad she'd brought an extra memory card with her. Not only did she get photos of the shoe giveaway. She got to take photos of their donation of food and other supplies they'd brought along with them. The head of the orphanage was also grateful. They also donated a few soccer balls, and the children played outside with them.

"This is amazing," she told Matt as he came to stand next to her.

"I could move back here in a heartbeat," he said.

"Back?"

"Yeah, my sister wasn't the only one who came here. I spent three years over here with the Peace Corps. It was what sealed it for me to go into ministry. I wanted to not only help them physically, but I wanted to minister to their spirits. They have such wonderful spirits. The people here get into your heart."

"So what happened? And remember, you are talking to a reporter," she said with a smile.

"I went back home and started seminary. I met someone. You know the story. I fell in love and got married."

"You're married?"

His smile faded as a pained expression crossed his face.

"About two years after we got married, we were expecting our first child. She was on the way to an appointment for a sonogram. We were going to find out if we were having a boy or girl. I was going to meet her at the office. A driver ran a red light. They were killed instantly. We were having a boy."

He stared at the orphans.

"That was seven years ago."

"I'm sorry."

"So now, I live my life for Him," he said.

He touched her arm.

"Thanks for asking. People don't let me talk. They don't ask, but sometimes, I want to remember my wife without feeling guilty, and I like to think about what I once had. She was a great woman. I miss her every day."

Matt walked away and joined in their game of soccer.

Everyone on this trip had a story. In a couple of days, a new shift of workers would come in. Each of them had a story as well. The next team to arrive would begin construction on an orphanage near the main church the group was affiliated with.

The orphanage wouldn't be a huge facility. They were expecting to have plenty of labor to get the building finished quickly. With no rain, they didn't have to worry about construction delays related to weather either.

Lisa changed out her lens and used a zoom to take photos of Matt playing ball with the children. He became alive and animated again as he kicked the ball around with them. Then, Lisa decided to do something else out of her character; she put her camera gear away and joined in the game with them.

Matt seemed surprised.

Lisa laughed.

"What? I need the full experience to be able to write about it," she said.

That evening Lisa uploaded several hundred images of the children, Matt and other team members. She sent a couple of photos to Jessie who was seven hours behind her. Jessie responded almost immediately.

"Guess who was waiting for me when I showed up at work today? Maybe, there's hope for you. I'd like to believe this," she wrote.

Lisa felt her heart skip as she read the note. Tom could be there in a few days. Her clues weren't too difficult. Matt noticed her face as she sat staring at her computer. She seemed shocked and happy at the same time.

"Is it worth sharing?" he asked.

"He's back home. He got home early. And he's following my clues. He figured out the first one and followed its direction to get the second. Maybe it was wisdom, after all?"

"I look forward to meeting him. And if you are interested, I've been told I'm good at marriage counseling. I actually have a degree in counseling as well as divinity. I have some practical experience in the subject as well. I wasn't married long, but it made me realize how every day is important. I urge my couples to look at the big picture.

There are several who were headed for divorce, but after counseling, they are still together. And they are happy."

"I learn something new about you all the time," she said.

She smiled and nodded.

"I'd love to take you up on the counseling. I hope it will be with my husband," she said.

"I got some good news, too."

Matt stood in the middle of the room. As he got the attention of everyone in the room, the door opened and a new member walked in. It was Jackson Devereux, the former wayward son. At 30, he was tall and good-looking with light brown hair. He was the youngest child of the Devereux clan of three daughters and one son. He didn't look like the son of one of the wealthiest men in town and a future Senator. He wore jeans and a torn T shirt with a rock band on the front of it and a red baseball cap.

"Great timing dude," Matt said to his brother-in-law who would be sharing a room with him for the duration of the trip. "Hey, everybody! I have great news, and Jack, you are just in time to hear it. They fixed the drill today and restarted on the well. We will be going back tomorrow, and we expect to see some water."

There was a cheer from the team, and Matt's face beamed. Lisa knew she had to get the photo of him and that expression once they discovered water. It would make a great shot.

"Now, everyone go to bed because we are leaving really early tomorrow morning."

Everyone laughed at Matt sending them to get some sleep, but they all knew the needed it. There weren't any objections.

Lisa tried to sleep. Her body clock had still not adjusted to the seven hour time difference, but that wasn't keeping her awake. She couldn't stop thinking about Tom. Despite what had happened in the most recent months, she still loved him deeply. Yes, she'd been angry and hurt, but she wasn't willing to walk away from their relationship. It had brought so much joy into their lives. This had been the longest they'd been apart since they were married and missing him was agony. She hoped it had been the same for him. About the time she'd fallen asleep, Matt began walking through the house, waking everyone up.

"We are hoping to strike water today," he said to the group after they'd gotten into the van. "We don't really have an agenda out there today. Lisa is probably the only one in the group who needs to be out there, but you deserve to see it and the faces of the people when they see the water. We do have some food we are taking out there. I know this is going to be a great day. I can feel it."

The sunrise over the African plain was breathtaking, and although she wasn't sure photographs of it would end up anywhere else except in her personal scrapbook, she snapped numerous pictures through her open van window.

When they arrived, they noticed a crowd gathered around. Even though they didn't speak the same language, it was obvious the villagers were excited. They knew water was coming to their thirsty land. The team had started on the drilling of the well the previous day once they'd replaced the broken part. Because of the severity of the drought, they knew they'd have to dig several hundred feet into the hard earth before they could find water.

Team members had a few extra soccer balls which they brought with them in hopes of engaging the children. Matt and Jackson, Mr. Devereux's son, showed off their dribbling skills and played with the children. Images of Jackson with children would help earn Lisa's paycheck.

"Hey Matt!" the drilling foreman called out.

Matt stopped playing and motioned for the children to follow him as he rushed toward the drill. Lisa moved quickly and got pushed past a couple of people to get the shots. Water began to flow out of the freshly dug well. There were shouts, and several people began to dance. Others began to cry. There was a lot of hugging, and Lisa was in a photo-snapping frenzy. Later that evening, Lisa uploaded her images onto her computer. She clicked through the images, amazed at some of the photos she had no idea she'd gotten. There was one image she really wanted to see, and there it was. She had a photo of Matt's reaction; it was priceless. She wished she could have as much excitement and pure joy in her life as she saw in his face. He really did care about helping these people, and his compassion was contagious. The other photos of the close-ups of facial expressions when they hit water told her story; what words could she come up with to tell it any better?

It had been a successful day – tiring but successful. She wondered if Tom was finding any success with is mission.

Tom was perplexed by the key he found around the bear's neck.

It was a small key. It wouldn't fit in a door. It looked like it went to some type of box. He examined her jewelry box on the dresser. She also had a freestanding piece of furniture for her jewelry. As he looked, he noticed one of its drawers had a keyhole. It fit, and inside the drawer was another clue, written on a black piece of cardstock in red, white and blue. She'd glued glitter onto the card as well.

"On that night, they lit up the sky, but when you popped a question, my heart did fly."

He knew exactly where that clue would lead him. With the short November daylight, he knew he'd have to wait in the morning to travel to the lake to find the next clue.

That night, he placed the ugly pink bear and the clues on her pillow next to him.

"I'm one step closer," he said as he tried to sleep.

13

It was hard to think of July in November, but Tom set his mind on that Independence Day and the fireworks over the lake.

Lisa's two favorite holidays were Christmas and Independence Day. They sounded like an odd combination, but Lisa's birthday was July 4. She felt as though the entire country celebrated her on that day, and she loved fireworks' displays.

They spent part of the day with her mother before heading to the lake with some friends. There was a public area not too far from the marina where the fireworks would be set off. They were able to find an open grill and cooked hot dogs. After they ate, Lisa and her girlfriends soaked up some rays while the guys conspired to dunk them in the water. When they least expected, the guys picked up their girlfriends and ran headlong into the water with the girls kicking and screaming the whole way. Lisa's perfect hairstyle being ruined by lake water didn't make her happy, but as it dried, it curled on its own into long ringlets. He wondered why she spent all that time primping and curling when her natural hair was so beautiful.

Tom had been planning his proposal for weeks. He'd wanted to take her out for her birthday, but she wanted to see the fireworks instead. He wanted it to be romantic. He'd thought about a fancy dinner and getting on one knee in the restaurant. He thought about gathering friends around and making the grand announcement in front of them all. Of course, that would have been embarrassing if she'd said no.

As they spent the day together, he realized he would never have the perfect moment. That evening, boats began to converge on the area where they'd spent the day in preparation for the fireworks' show. Lisa's fair skin had burned during the day despite sunscreen, but she was determined to stay for the fireworks. As the reds, greens and other vivid hues exploded across the night sky, Tom turned to Lisa.

"Lisa, would you marry me?"

She gave him a puzzled look.

"What?" she yelled. She couldn't hear him over the sounds of the bursting pyrotechnics.

"Lisa Miller, will you marry me?" he yelled back as the fireworks ended to huge cheers and applause.

"I can't hear you!"

He yelled it one last time.

"Lisa Miller, will you marry me?"

She heard him that time, and so did everyone else surrounding them as the fireworks had come to an end and the applause had died down. People near them turned.

Their friends seemed surprised, and everyone around them waited for her answer.

"Yes, Tom Kinsey, I will marry you."

Their friends yelled and cheered as did the other people who were nearby.

He kissed her, and then he realized he didn't have the ring with him.

"What's wrong?"

"I have a ring. It's just not here."

"It's fine. I don't need a ring," she said as she kissed him again.

Things were much simpler then, or were they? He wondered about this journey Lisa was walking him through. What had happened over the years? He thought they had had a good marriage. It wasn't perfect. There were things that pushed them to the brink, but they always returned and held on to one another.

And as he thought back to Christine, he wondered what was special about her. Could he blame everything on his father? Could he blame it on the alcohol? He couldn't really think of anything except she was attractive and didn't make any attempts to hide that she was interested in him. There had been two other women he'd worked closely with who had this same profile. He made it clear to them he was married, and he wouldn't cheat on his wife. With Christine, it wasn't that he'd fallen in love. He knew it was physical attraction, and he was grateful Gene was with him on his last night in London. Was he like his father? He didn't think he was. Gene was right. He'd pulled away from Lisa instead of pulling her close. He liked the idea that at the age of 47, he had a younger, attractive woman who was interested in him.

The 45-minute drive to the lake caused him to think about his alcoholic father who abused him and his mother. His dad told him to take his punishment like a man. He was taught never to cry. Real mean didn't cry. His mother cried though. In the moments after he told Lisa what he'd done, he saw his mother's expression written across her face. He had to come to terms with what he'd done. Yes, he could say that seeing Courtney die in the wreck had triggered those unresolved feelings of helplessness. Yes, he could point to the alcohol for weakening his defenses. Ultimately, he had to look at himself and bear the consequences for what he'd done.

He'd do whatever it took to get Lisa back. If it meant following her every clue, then he'd do it. Lisa was too important to him.

Tom knew he needed to talk to someone to. Gene was great, but because Tom was his employer, he didn't tell him everything. He needed a professional. How was he going to do that?

He wasn't sure about this new relationship with God either. He had prayed with Gene, and he felt different, lighter, new. That joyful feeling left when he discovered his wife was gone. How could God help him with these problems he was facing? He wasn't sure he knew the answer. He did feel a sense of empowerment after he prayed and poured the alcohol down the drain. Strange, he hadn't even thought about having a drink over the past couple of days. Maybe there was something to this prayer thing after all.

"Dear God, I want to learn to pray. I know I messed up. I need your help. I need Lisa back," he whispered.

Tom traveled to the public picnic area near a ridge of pine trees and small sandy beach area. It wasn't too far off the main road. On a November's day right after Thanksgiving, there wasn't any traffic, and there were no people at the site.

Where would she have hidden the next clue?

He started at the covered picnic area. It had a roof and some wooden support beams with a concrete floor. It was nothing special. He searched near the trash cans and then looked underneath the picnic tables. After getting on his hands and knees for the first four, he finally found an envelope in a plastic bag and duct-taped to the underside of a bench.

"Immense pressure turns coal into a diamond, and an oyster turns irritation into a pearl. I couldn't think of a great rhyme here for some reason, but I do believe what could have ended this for us could be used to make our marriage a beautiful jewel for all to see. Do you remember where you gave me my ring? Go there for your next clue."

He laughed as he stared at the paper. There were several numbers listed as well.

"Oh Lisa, you always told it like it is."

Where he gave her the engagement ring wasn't too far from where he was standing. A few days after the fireworks show on the lake they came back but to a different spot. He would have to drive to another park. They were planning a picnic just the two of them. It was a quiet Monday afternoon. There were some people at the lake, but not as many as on the weekend. The lake levels were really low because of a drought, and they were in the middle of a blistering heat wave. They'd had triple digits for almost two weeks with no rain in sight to break through. Officials advised people to stay indoors, but Tom and Lisa were counting on some areas of shade.

"You've never been to the peak?" Lisa asked him.

"No, what's the peak?"

"Come on. You have to see it. I can't describe it."

Lisa grabbed his hand and started their walk. She was wearing a one-piece red bathing suit and a pair of jean shorts. Thinking there might be a chance that he was going to dunk her in the lake again, she forgot about regular hair regimen and stuffed her hair under a baseball cap.

They had started their day at one of the beach areas, and the heat had become unbearable. A trek to the peak required a pass through the woods, and at least among all the towering Georgia pines, there was a bit of a reprieve from the weather, but not much.

"You would pick the hottest day of the year to decide to go hiking," he said.

"We are almost there. It's worth it. Besides, that's why we brought canteens along. We will be fine."

Just then, they came to a clearing. There aren't any mountains where they lived, but there are lots of hills. From the point they called "the peak," they could peer over the lake and see the terrain. The lake seemed calm from their vantage point.

"It's beautiful, but it's not as beautiful as you," he said, pulling her close to him to kiss him. The baseball cap got in the way so he pushed it off her head. He wanted to be able to touch her hair anyway.

"I know I asked you this a couple of days ago. It was impulsive. I want to do it right."

He pulled a box out of his shorts' pocket and fell to one knee. He opened the box and presented it to her.

"Lisa, will you marry me?"

"Of course, I will."

He placed the ring on her finger. It was a half-carat round solitaire.

She gasped. Her eyes widened and her jaw dropped.

"It's gorgeous," she said as she dropped to her knees to be at his level. She wrapped her arms around his neck and began to kiss him.

"This is a small diamond, but I promise you one day it will grow into a much larger one. I pro-"

She cut him off by kissing him again.

"I couldn't ask for anything more beautiful. I love you so much," she said.

"I promise to get you a larger one," he said. He placed his hands around her waist, and he kissed her lips.

"We have our whole lives together, and I don't care about the size of the diamond," she said. "I only want you."

"I'm counting on our whole lives together. I never thought I'd meet anyone like you. I love you, Lisa."

"I love you, Tom. I think I've loved you from the first moment we bumped heads," she said and giggled. "As embarrassing as it was at the time, it will always be one of my favorite memories."

Tom was jolted back to reality as a deer jumped in front of him on the country road. He slammed on brakes to avoid hitting the animal and lurched forward into the steering wheel. He sat for a few minutes to catch his breath and stared ahead of him. The memory of day and emotions it brought with it were so vivid. He could almost taste Lisa's lips and feel her breath on his face. He missed her so much. These clues were driving him crazy. He wanted to get through them all so he could touch her face and kiss her lips again. He wanted to hold her in his arms and wake up in the morning with her next to him.

He tried to think where she could possibly hide a clue there in the middle of trees and grass. He parked and made the trek to the peak. He couldn't get his picture of Lisa out of his mind. She planned it that way. Even after all of the years, that was one special day they often talked about. He looked at the clue again. He walked around confused for several minutes.

"Please help me figure out this clue," he prayed in desperation.

While he was contemplating the numbers, his phone rang. It was Gene. He was surprised he had any reception in such a remote location.

"Any word from Lisa?"

"You could say that."

"She called?"

"No, she left me some bread crumbs, and I'm following them."

"Okay. Well if you need anything, Kathy and I are here to help."

"Thanks."

When he ended the call, he hit the touchscreen on his phone too many times, and he pulled up an app he'd never seen before. It was a compass, and it brought up the coordinates of his location. They followed the same pattern as the numbers she'd written on the clue. He was looking for a specific coordinate, and it was close by.

"I'd call that a quick answer to prayer. Thank You," said Tom as he began to walk around using the compass on his phone as a guide. He headed towards the center of the area they called the peak. It was a higher hill. It definitely wasn't a mountain, and there was a large grassy expanse. He kept moving until he saw the exact numbers she'd written down. He noticed several rocks. He moved them and began to dig. He didn't go far until he found another plastic bag with a Christmas card inside it. It featured a glittery, snow-covered church. She wrote in silver marker on this one.

"Dear Tom, I'm impressed. I was really concerned you might not find this one. I'll make the next one easy for you, or will I? Go to the place of true love's first kiss. If you miss the pastor, just look for Alice."

Also included with the card was a wedding photo. He sat on the grass and stared at the photo. Of course, he'd kissed her before they got married, but that first kiss as husband and wife was magical. He'd often remarked to her how special it was to him. He even referred to it as "true love's first kiss." He was never sure of the reason he thought that. He recalled the flutter he felt. He didn't think many men would admit something so hopelessly romantic, but there was a tender side to Tom only Lisa knew. As he sat there on the grass in the cool of November, he knew he'd let that part of him slip away over the years. He'd let the romance die. Instead of cherishing her as he'd promised to do on his wedding day, he'd taken her and their relationship for granted, and he knew it. He realized he'd shifted some blame onto her in his mind. She was too involved with work and the kids. She spent too much time with the arts community. She wasn't home enough. Those were simply excuses. She always said that it took two people to make a marriage work.

He began walking toward the car, and once he was out of danger of tripping over tree roots, he started to run. He had to get the next clue and driving to the church would take another 30 to 45 minutes.

They married near the Christmas after she graduated college. Lisa had started working at the newspaper her senior year as a clerk at night and transitioned into a full-time feature reporter position as soon as she graduated. Tom graduated the year before her. He got a job in sales, and of course, he was a natural. Since Lisa's mother couldn't provide a wedding, Tom told her he would make sure she had her fairytale dream wedding. Lisa had always loved theater, and her flair for the dramatic was evident in the setting. Since they lived in the South, they'd never seen a Christmas covered in snow and ice. Christmas always looked pretty covered in white in pictures. Lisa had always loved the thought of a white Christmas so she decided to transform the quaint little church into her own winter wonderland, even though it was about 60 degrees that December day.

He had no idea of what the church really looked like. She'd completely taken over the décor. The altar was filled with white poinsettias and arrangements of white roses, carnations and any white flower she could find. There were so many of them Tom thought she must have depleted the entire stock of white flowers in the city and several surrounding ones. There were several Christmas trees of varying sizes decorated only with twinkling white Christmas lights and white ornaments. In front of the altar was an arch covered in white tulle, white roses and carnations and intertwined with hundreds of the tiny white lights. A dozen free-standing candelabra were also decorated with the lights. At one point in the ceremony, the lights were dimmed so the soft light on the altar provided most of the lighting.

Lisa's tailor-made long-sleeved satin wedding dress had a faux fur neckline and cuffs. There were rhinestones embedded into the waistline to create a belt. Tom had thought the dress resembled a formal coat in its design, but he didn't say that. It was elegant, and she was breathtaking in it. She wore her chestnut hair in a partial bun with loose curls which cascaded past her shoulders. She was a classic beauty.

He stared at her from the moment she entered the chapel and walked down the white rose-petal covered runner. She walked the aisle alone; she didn't have another male relative to give her away.

When she reached the end of the aisle, she smiled at him. She truly looked like his angel in the white gown and beautifully curled hair. He fumbled over his vows and almost missed several cues from the minister because he was mesmerized with her. She had to prompt him by touching the side of his face when he was given the go-ahead to kiss his bride. He placed his right hand on her cheek and gently caressed it as he slowly kissed her. The kiss was dreamlike. It felt different. He was never able to fully explain what the difference was, but there was a kaleidoscope of butterflies in his stomach that were set into motion at that precise moment when their lips touched for the first time as husband and wife. He couldn't remember a happier time than when the minister announced them as "Mr. and Mrs. Thomas David Kinsey."

Tom pulled up in the parking lot of the old church. He sat and stared at the building for a few minutes. Their 25th wedding anniversary was in less than two weeks.

Although all of the memories she'd selected so far had come

from events that took place at least 25 years ago, it felt as if they'd only taken place in the past few weeks. The cheesy poems brought back specific images and feelings from those days. They stirred something inside of him. He knew he had always loved her. There was no one else in the world he wanted to be with. He had to get to her before their fast-approaching anniversary.

The picturesque white chapel with its steeple sat atop a hill. There were several large oak trees on the property, and there was an old cemetery as well. There were no cars in the parking lot when he arrived. He walked around to the back of the church, where an office might be. He knocked, but there was no answer.

Look for Alice, the note said. Who was Alice?

Lisa was also into history, and the two of them had visited several cemeteries together. Actually, she was the one who visited them, and she dragged him along. She went for the architecture, she said and to take photographs. The older graves often had unusual carvings and epitaphs. She'd tell him the modern ones just didn't have style.

There weren't many graves in the churchyard. Tom walked swiftly, looking at the names on the markers. Was an Alice buried there? No. He walked toward the back of the church and noticed a mausoleum. He didn't see that before. It had a locked wrought iron gate. He walked up the steps to the gate. Over the gate in the granite was carved the last name Habersham. There was a plaque to the right of the entrance with the names of the entombed. One of them was Alice.

Tom shook the gate. It was locked tight. He felt inside the gate. Nothing except a spider web. Maybe she had hid the clue somewhere around the mausoleum. He jumped off the steps and continued his search. He walked around the building, concentrating on the lower part of it.

When he reached the back corner, he noticed a cinderblock propped up against it.

He moved the block and an enveloped sealed in a plastic bag and taped to the side.

"You're almost finished. I've never been much of a poet so I'll revert to prose. Go to Christ Church and find Rev Matthew Davis' secretary. She will have an envelope for you. It might be your last, but then again, it might not," she wrote.

Christ Church? he thought.

He'd never been to the Christ Church, and as far as he knew, neither had she. He didn't even know where it was. He found the address on his phone. It would take a while to drive there. He wondered if anyone would be there on a Saturday. He called the number, but there was no answer. He had a few hours of daylight left; he decided to take a chance someone might be there and not near the phone. When he arrived, he noticed there were two men raking leaves in front of the church readying it for the morning service.

"Excuse me, is the church secretary here?" he asked one of them.

"No, Miss Grace doesn't work on Saturdays, and she's gone to visit her sister in Alabama for Thanksgiving. She won't be back until Monday morning," the man replied.

Tom nodded and headed home. He felt his heart sink. Monday seemed like an eternity.

14

The end of the first group's tour in Africa was almost complete. They gathered for one final meal together and a special time of prayer.

"I want to thank each one of you for making the sacrifice to be away from your family and friends at Thanksgiving and for giving up the Black Friday sales back home," said Matt.

His shopping joke received a chorus of laughs.

One of the members stood up.

"Could I say something?" she asked.

He nodded.

"This was amazing for me. I will never forget the looks on the faces of those people as they saw the water coming out of the well – and how they hugged me," she started to cry with the memory.

Others in the room nodded; some clapped.

"Lisa has put together a photo slideshow for all of you to watch," said Matt. "This will be up at the website, and when we return, we will put it on CD for you."

Everyone gathered around the table to see the computer show. Although it was only about 10 minutes long, there wasn't a dry eye in the room by the time it was completed. Even Jackson, the wayward son, who Lisa was convinced had turned a new page in his life, had tears streaming down his cheeks.

Matt stood up and turned the lights back on. He took a

couple of minutes to compose himself.

"This is what it's all about," he said. "Making a difference in the lives of people who can never repay you."

He paused and wiped his eyes.

"I want to pray a blessing over all of you as you head home in the morning, and we want to pray for the other group arriving tomorrow afternoon. We are so thankful to God who has been so generous to us on this trip," he said. "With our next group, we will begin construction on the orphanage and school. It should go quickly. Another team from another part of our state will be arriving at the end of the week as well. We're really excited about all of this."

Jackson also stood up.

"I'm not going to make a speech. If my dad has his way, I'll be making a lot of those in the coming years."

He paused for everyone to laugh. They knew what plans had been made for the Golden Boy Devereux.

"I just want to thank you for treating me like a member of the team. It's been hard work, but my wife, who will be joining me after Christmas, and my brother-in-law have shown me by example what it's like to love people. I really want to serve people."

He stopped and looked at Lisa.

"Lisa, don't include this, but I wonder if there's another place where I could make an impact other than government. It's just a thought for now. Washington is so full of red tape."

Lisa smiled and nodded. She would keep Jackson's secret because it could throw a wrench into her book plans. She had so much information. She'd obtained much more than she ever used for a single newspaper article. She contemplated how she was going to turn it all into a book. The next morning would be time off for her to collect her thoughts. If she could stop thinking about Tom, she might be able to get somewhere.

Matt had driven with the team to the airport that morning.

Jackson was up early for his morning cup of coffee when Lisa walked into the kitchen.

"So when are you going to tell your father?" she asked.

Jackson laughed.

"I talked too much last night."

"Maybe. I don't know your dad as well as you do, but I do know he's shrewd. You might be able to fool him for a little while but not forever. I also know he's very set in his ways, and he always gets his way," she said.

"That sums him up."

Jackson looked into his cup of coffee for a few minutes.

"I admit I had my wild days, but from the time I was a kid, he wanted me in politics. In high school, I had to run for office of every club I was in so I could learn something about parliamentary procedure. I hated it all. I majored in political science and partying in college," he said.

Lisa laughed.

"So I've heard."

"Then, my dad cut me off from his money. Probably a good idea. I got a job, but I continued to party. And then, there was the infamous drunken brawl in the bar with my arrest that ended up as the lead story on every news outlet in town except your newspaper where it was buried somewhere near the obituaries. Then, the charges were 'mysteriously' dropped. You, me and the entire state knew there was no mystery when it came to those charges being dropped."

Lisa nodded.

"That's when I started to take a look at myself," he said. "I didn't want to just be Grayson Devereux's son with a trust fund and a silver spoon. I did want the money - don't get me wrong. Making it without him and his connections was hard. I think he told everyone in town not to hire me. So, I decided to play his game a little. He wanted me to get married, and that was the best decision I ever made."

"How did you meet Matt's sister?"

"Well, that's one of those stories that never made it into the paper," he said and shook his head.

"I have a feeling there are a lot of those."

"And you would be correct. My father has paid for more repairs to bars than you will ever know. And don't even get me started on the private parties. I was carried out of a few of those too. I went out one night and got into a scuffle at a bar. I needed some stitches so I went to the ER. There was a pretty nurse named Jamie. I wanted to take her out simply because she was so beautiful. She ignored me on that night. Good idea. I found out who she was and after several months of me pestering her, she agreed to go out with me."

Jackson smiled.

"Persuading her to marry me took a little longer. My reputation damaged me on that. I had to do repair work in her eyes first. Jamie's a lot like Matt. She's got a fantastic personality, but she's rock when it comes to what she believes."

"So if you don't want to go into government, what do you want to do?" she asked.

"I want to head this charity my dad started, and Jamie and I want to move to Africa. She studied nursing so she could use it in a third world nation not in an ER back home," he said. "But that's totally off the record. I have to figure out how to get Dad to agree and not pull his money."

He grinned with the last statement. Lisa nodded.

When Matt returned about an hour later, he found Lisa at her computer, working on the website and blog. The newspaper had been promoting the info on the trip, and it was getting a lot of hits. Lisa had asked for it to be kept anonymous until she knew the outcome of her plan. Instead of a reporter byline, it said "from staff reports."

"So, how long before the other group comes in?" Lisa asked.

"I'll head back to the airport in about six hours," he said.

"You get part of a day off anyway."

"Jackson and I have some things to talk about. And there are things his dad wants to see on your blog."

"Yes, I got an email – a rather lengthy one."

Matt laughed.

"Not surprising. Jackson has a few things his dad wants accomplished. While Jackson has plans of his own, he's going along with his dad's plans right now. As you know, that is completely off the record."

"Of course."

"Lisa, can I ask you a personal question?"

"You really know how to take a person off-guard," she said and tried to laugh.

"Sorry about that. I believe in getting straight to the point."

"So, I can tell. I guess it all depends on the question you want to ask."

"Actually, I have more than one question. I know I'm not your pastor, but I care about what you are going through," he said.

He made a cup of coffee and sat at the table next to her.

"I was skeptical when Mr. Devereux said a reporter would be coming along with us. I've met a few, and they aren't always like you."

Lisa nodded.

"I guess that's good."

"It is, and I really like you. I want to see things work out for you and your husband because I believe you love him."

"Okay. I appreciate that."

"Have you talked to anyone about this?"

Lisa looked confused.

"What do you mean?"

"Have you talked to anyone about what you are going through with your husband?"

"No, not really."

"I can tell. You have some walls built. I know the situation is difficult, but those walls are not good."

"I don't know who to trust. Working for a newspaper as long as I have and seeing how people have complete disregard for their word has made me leery of people. I don't believe what people tell me, and I know the best way to keep a secret is to not tell anyone."

"I understand that, but do you have anyone you've confided in?"

"Not completely, no. People know only what they need to know, and Tom is the only one who needs to know everything."

"He doesn't even know everything. What are you doing to him?"

"I'm making him prove he still loves me."

"Sounds like a harsh test."

"He's put me through a harsh test," Lisa clenched her jaw and squinted at Matt. "I didn't ask for this."

"Tell me what you are doing."

"I told you. He likes challenges. He likes clues and mysteries."

"So what's the point of your game?"

"I also told you it wasn't a game to me. Each clue points to a special memory the two of us hold. He goes to the spot of those memories. They reignite something in him, and he comes here."

"Then, what happens?"

Lisa was shocked by the question.

"Happily ever after?" he prodded. "Or have your problems magically vanished?"

"No probably not, but at least if I know he loves me, we can work this out."

"Why didn't you stay home and wait?"

"He told me he was leaving me. He went to England for a month without giving me a return date. Although he hinted about coming back to the city, I don't know if he planned on coming home," Lisa paused as she wiped away a few tears that trickled down her cheeks. "Besides, this trip to Africa was my one real opportunity to do what I thought God wanted me to do years ago."

Now, it was Matt's turn to be a little confused.

"You had asked if I was a woman of faith. I used to be until I met Tom. I remember telling you I went on a couple of mission trips as a teenager; then, I went to college. My dad died. My mother's and my life changed. I put my missionary hopes and dreams on the shelf. Tom didn't see that as part of our lives, and I loved Tom more than I loved the idea of becoming a missionary."

Her voice trailed off.

"God was never really a part of our lives either. We took the children to church at Christmas and Easter, but that was about it. We did the do-gooder type things, but something started pulling at my heart. It was like you told me. Your trip here with the Peace Corps led you to want to be in the mission field. Something led me here, and it wasn't Mr. Devereux."

Lisa looked down.

"If you'd asked me when I was 17, where I'd be 30 years later. It would be here where I am today, but the path I walked down to get here would have been completely different."

"Lisa, I think you need to forgive someone."

"I've already forgiven Tom."

"I don't mean Tom. I mean Lisa."

Lisa raised an eyebrow.

"I don't understand."

"Yes, you need to forgive yourself because you feel like you've let God down."

Lisa began to cry. She knew he was right. She carried a lot of guilt of that one nagging thought.

"As much as I love Tom, there were so many times when I felt like I'd made a mistake in marrying him."

Matt gave her some tissues.

"I should have done so many things differently."

"You can't go back, but you are here now."

"What if Tom doesn't want this?"

"Speaking of Tom - are you sure you have you forgiven him? You can't start a new life with him if you don't forgive him."

Lisa continued to cry. She knew she hadn't dealt with any of the emotions. She'd said she'd forgiven Tom, but in her heart, she was still angry with him. She hadn't released all of the emotions.

"And you don't forgive him because he deserves it. You forgive him to release yourself from the jail of unforgiveness."

"What are you talking about?"

"Oh yeah, I forgot you don't go to my church. You missed that sermon. It was really good," he said and chuckled.

"I guess you need to fill me in."

"I spoke a couple of weeks ago about how the holidays are a good time to forgive your annoying relatives," he said.

She nodded.

"I see."

"No, you don't. When you hold unforgiveness and anger inside of you, it's like holding onto venom. You have to let it go, or it will turn into an acid that will eat you from the inside out. I also pointed out some scientific studies that proved this point along with the New Testament and the words of Jesus," he said with a smile.

Lisa nodded her head and tried to smile.

"If you hold this poison, you will eventually pour it on him, and it will end what's left of your marriage. I can promise you that," he said.

Matt stood up and touched her arm.

"I gave you a lot to think about. If you need to talk to me, you can trust me. I don't share information with people, and I have no time for gossip. But I do have time for people who are interested in being helped and making their situation better."

"Thank you."

"It's what I do. My job doesn't stop when I'm not at the church."

He left the room, and Lisa buried her face in her hands. He was right. She needed to forgive Tom, and she needed to forgive herself. Even though she loved Tom, she'd always wondered what it would have been like if she'd never bumped into him that day. Not only was she angry at him for Christine, but she was angry at him for taking her out of the plan she had wanted for her life. She hadn't realized it until then. She wasn't supposed to write that story; another reporter was, but the other student had a family emergency arise. Lisa called Tom the day before to rearrange the schedule.

But then again, maybe, she was where she was supposed to have been all along. After all, she was in the mission field in Africa, as she'd always dreamed. It just hadn't happened how she thought it would happen.

She did love Tom. She did believe him when he said what he did about Christine,

and she did want him in her life forever. But she also wanted what she had in the beginning before she ever met Tom. She wondered if she could have it all.

"Let him come here and let this touch his heart," she prayed.

15

Tom gathered all of the clues so far and put them in one location. He put the hot pink bear and the photographs with them. He wanted to give them to her. He wanted to prove himself to her.

He spent most of Sunday alone, thinking about the clues she'd left him and reliving those memories to fan the feelings he had for her. Brittany called to tell him how fantastic her ski trip had been and asked to speak with her mother. Tom didn't like to lie so he said Lisa was not at home and her phone was not operational. The battery was completely dead so it wasn't a complete lie, was it? He told Spencer the same thing. He felt guilty for not being upfront with either of them, but he hoped he would never have to tell them about what he and Lisa were going through.

Gene also called.

"Have you come to the bottom of the mystery?"

"Not completely, but I understand what's she doing. She's clever, and all of this has made me realize how much we once meant to each other. We've both let things slip away. If she's gone to this much trouble, then she's not ready to give up on us either. I have to go to Christ Church in the morning."

"What's at Christ Church?"

"I don't know, but the pastor's secretary does."

"Are you sure about all of this?"

"I know Lisa, and today, I'm getting my clothes washed and

packed. I'll be seeing her again soon. And Gene, I'm going to be taking some time off. I want you to be in charge while I'm gone. I'll let you know the details."

The reasons Tom fell in love with Lisa hadn't changed over the years. While their relationship had gone through its own evolution with the marriage, addition of children, changes in careers, loss of parents and the moving on of children, Tom and Lisa were the same at the core of their beings. She had blossomed, growing from an insecure and shy young adult into someone well aware of her gifts and talents and confident in how to use them. She took on the roles of motherhood and being a wife in stride. She did her job as a reporter well and overall she was a remarkable person. He loved her more now than he did when he first married her.

He was grateful for this experiment. As he focused on the good memories they shared together, he wasn't as haunted by the painful memories of his father, and he didn't need anything to drown his pain.

He had no idea what time a church office might open so he arrived a few minutes before 9 a.m. on Monday. He didn't really notice the church on his visit a few days before. He saw the structure was an historic church in an older part of town. It was a Victorian gothic building with a tall spire and stained glass windows. The front doors weren't unlocked, but he didn't think they would be. He walked around the back and found a door bell. He waited for several minutes and rang again. A woman in her late 50s opened the door and looked out.

"I'm Tom Kinsey. My wife, Lisa, told me to come here and talk to the Rev. Matt Davis' secretary," he said.

"I've been expecting you," she said.

"Did you have a nice visit with your sister over Thanksgiving, Miss Grace?" he asked.

She smiled at him.

"As a matter of fact, I did, Mr. Kinsey. Thank you," she said.

He walked through the back of the old building through a

corridor. The wooden floors squeaked as he walked behind her.

"Historic building," he said attempting to make small talk.

"Oh yes, it was built in 1876. All of the floors are original, and so are the stained glass windows."

"It's beautiful."

"Yes, I love coming in here to work," she said.

She walked into an office and went behind a desk, pulled out what looked like a greeting card.

"Am I allowed to ask you any questions?" he asked.

"You can ask all the questions you'd like, but I probably can't answer them."

"Did she tell you anything?"

She smiled.

"Only that you're almost there."

Tom nodded and followed as she walked him back to the entrance.

"Your wife seems like a lovely lady, and she has a good heart."

"Yes, she does. Thank you."

Tom stared at the envelope. When he got inside the car, he opened it. Inside was one of the promotional postcards for the African mission. It had a photograph of Matt next to the well-drilling machine on it and said, "Support water wells in Kenya with Rev. Davis."

Africa? he thought. He was confused. There was also a brief note.

"Poetry time is over. Go look inside my hope chest at the foot of the bed. The key to its lock is in my closet hidden in a shoe box marked Lion's Den. There's a packet for you inside the chest."

He was still reeling from the postcard. Had she ever said anything about Africa? He couldn't remember. He rushed home as quickly as he could without running any lights or breaking the sound barrier. He knew that was Lisa at Heathrow. This explained it. Once inside the house, he headed straight for the closet and key. He opened the chest. There was a thick brown 9-inch by 12-inch envelope awaiting him. He poured its contents on the bed.

There was another greeting card envelope plus a stack of photographs with a rubber band securing them. There was a map of Africa and Lisa's itinerary. He opened the card first. It was a 25th anniversary card.

"Dear Tom, If you are reading this, then you've found all the clues. In my heart, I knew you would. I'd always imagined a big party or something special for our 25th anniversary. I'm not sure what it will hold this year, or if we'll even be together. As you've probably guessed, I'm in Africa now. Yes, that's right - Africa. I've left several photographs for you."

He picked up the pictures and began to look through them. He recognized Lisa as a teenager. Brittany looked just like her. On the back were written the names of countries and other people in the photographs. She looked so happy in the photos.

"I made a few missions trips when I was a teen. It was what I wanted to do with my life. I wanted to serve God and serve people. Then, things changed. I had to come back from the school I attended as a freshman. My dad died. I met you. I put some of my dreams on hold, or I buried them. I'm not sure which. Recently, the opportunity arose to make those dreams come true and to help some people who desperately need it."

She told him all the details of the drilling project- from the people involved to the books she would write.

"My hope is that on this quest I've sent you on, you've rediscovered the passion you had for me and the love that brought us together. I know it made me feel close to you planning it all out. I relived each of those memories. At each location, I could feel you there with me. It seems as though it was all only yesterday. I miss you. I miss us. I hope this letter explains most of it. I can answer the rest of your questions in person. I've left my itinerary with you."

He looked through the brochures about the drilling project. There were photographs and a few letters from the church. She had also printed out a page from the newspaper's website featuring information on the upcoming blog and coverage. He went to Lisa's computer. He had looked on it before to see if there was anything that stood out, but there wasn't anything. He logged onto the paper's website. He saw the photographs of the children playing ball with Matt. He saw the joy on the faces of the people at the well.

Tom had thought about making a difference a lot over the past few months especially after watching Courtney die. While he and Lisa had given money to charity and she had volunteered a lot, he always wondered if he could really say if his life made a difference to anyone else. Taking water to people in a land where there was no water - that could definitely make a difference, and there were building projects as well.

The whole reason Tom got into real estate and development was a summer job he'd had when he was in high school. He worked construction two summers doing manual labor for a company building new neighborhoods. He was amazed with how quickly the structures seemed to go up. There was a level of pride he had felt even though he'd only played a small role in building them. He often rode past those neighborhoods and recalled those hot summers.

Was there another plan for him too?

He had felt like a new person since that night when he prayed with Gene. He didn't know how to describe it. He knew he was getting a second chance. He had a second chance with God, and he was hoping for a second chance with Lisa. He saw his life in a different light.

"Show me the way," he prayed quietly.

While he was seated at the computer, he began searching for flights. Their anniversary was in a little more than a week. Should he wait to go then? There were no direct flights. The flights with the fewest stops were closer to their anniversary; otherwise, there were lengthy layovers in New York and London.

Should his arrival be a surprise? He imagined greeting her when she least expected it. But if he waited, would it backfire?

16

Lisa tried to keep her mind off Tom, and the next group's arrival kept her busy. She was thankful for the long van ride with people who had a contagious enthusiasm. By now, this new group had seen the website and the photographs of the people getting water from the well, and that's all they could talk about on the way to the village. They couldn't wait to be part of bringing life into other dry and thirsty regions.

While the bulk of this group's experience would be to start the building process, they were traveling to a village so they could interact with the people there, and they could see how what they were doing would impact the region. With the building, they wouldn't be interacting too much with the people who would be using the facility. The central part of the orphanage would be constructed by year's end. It wouldn't be anything elaborate. It was designed with function and efficiency in mind.

As with the other group, the members of this group reiterated why they were making the trip. Lisa could relate to some of them. There were a few people who felt life had passed them by, and they wanted to do something significant to help others. Lisa didn't say much, and it was difficult for her to take notes because of the terrain the vehicle encountered. She used her recorder to get bits and pieces of the conversations.

Matt noticed her distant look, but he had some information

he thought would cheer her.

Matt had already given team members instructions about what they would be doing in the villages. Each person had a task in helping with the drilling team. The team brought food along on this trip to distribute as well. Also, they brought some soccer balls because the children had no toys to play with. The balls meant a lot to them.

Through an interpreter, Matt told them about God's love for them and how the team was expressing that love to them by drilling wells in the land.

Crowd control was one function the team members could perform until the water began to flow. Everyone was curious about the process. They explained it as best they could, but the people wanted to get close.

The drilling team had already been working when the other members arrived. It wasn't too long before water was flowing freely. Once again, there were tears of joy. Lisa couldn't contain her feelings. It seemed like a perfect time to let the pent-up tears flow. She wondered if Tom had gotten through all of her clues. Was he on a flight? Would he be at the house when they returned? He hadn't emailed her. There had been no comments at the website. Was he gone forever? Was he angry for the chase? The waiting was agony as her mind played out each scenario – good and bad.

She recalled the old fisherman by the lake that one day. He told her everything would be okay. She wanted to believe it. As she snapped photographs and cried, she felt someone come up behind her. She stopped and turned to see Matt standing next to her. She wiped her tears.

"This breaks my heart in a good way every time I see it," she said. "I can't get over it."

"Yes, but I have a feeling there are some other things you are crying over," he said.

Lisa didn't want to look him in the eye. She raised the camera and started snapping photos again.

"I'm trying not to think about my problems. These people

have more problems than I could ever imagine. I'm blessed in comparison."

"I have some news you might find interesting."

Lisa was curious. She slowly took the camera down and looked at Matt. She raised an eyebrow. She was a little nervous at what he might say.

"Really?"

"I've wanted to tell you, but I didn't want to when other people were around."

"Okay. Well, this looks like your best shot."

"Tom stopped by the church."

A wave of relief passed over her face. Matt saw Lisa's first genuine smile since he'd met her.

"I was wondering what your smile looked like," he said.

"I've smiled here."

"Yes, but it's been forced."

She nodded.

"Did he say anything?"

"My secretary said he seemed anxious. He wanted to ask her questions, but he didn't. He was confused obviously. How many clues did he have to find to make it to the church?"

"Several, but he was almost finished. The final clues were at the house, and he would have found those once he went to the church."

"What's next?"

"I hope he comes here. Our 25th anniversary is soon – next week. I have told him I have an obligation here."

"What about your kids and Christmas? What if he doesn't come?"

Lisa's smile faded.

"I don't know."

"Lisa, have you forgiven him?"

Lisa took a deep breath and thought about that question for a moment. Then, she stared straight into Matt's eyes.

"I thought about everything you said before. It was hard, but yes, I have."

"Are you sure? You've made him prove himself by jumping through a lot of hoops."

"I know that's how it looks. I wasn't trying to punish him. I wanted him to remember everything. I love him. I'm willing to make this work, but I have to know he wants it too."

He smiled.

"Work out any anger you may have. If you really want to move on, you can't have a punishment mentality. He will never be able to make it up to you and punishing him will only push him away."

"I understand," she said softly. "Here I was thinking that I was coming to help you, and you've been the one to help me."

"That's my job," said Matt as he patted her on the back and walked back to the drill.

Tom was trying to decide his next move as he heard the doorbell ringing.

It was Gene.

"What's going on, buddy? You haven't answered your phone all day," he said as Tom let him in.

"What time is it?" he asked. He walked past Gene outside and glanced around. "When did it get dark?"

"You are out of it, aren't you?" Gene replied.

Tom walked back in and looked at Gene.

"Kathy sent you over?"

"Well, yes."

Tom grinned.

"I'm not surprised. Tell her Lisa's in Africa," Tom said casually as he walked past Gene toward his home office.

"Africa? Why?" asked a confused Gene.

Tom motioned for him to follow.

"I am putting it all together now."

Tom sat down at his desk, and Gene took the other chair in

the room. All of the clues were placed in front of him. Gene's mouth dropped.

"Sounds like someone really needed proof you meant what you said."

Tom nodded.

"And I owed it to her to prove it. It's the very least I could do," Tom replied. "What's your next move?"

"I'm checking flights to Nairobi now. I have made some stupid mistakes over the past several weeks, but this journey Lisa has taken me on," his voice trailed off. "I can't get to her fast enough. She made me remember why I fell in love with her, and I've thought of the times when she's been there for me. I've thought about the tough times. She didn't remind me of those. She reminded me of the good times, but it was in those dark times, when I always needed her, she was there. Why I didn't turn to her now I don't know. Maybe she could have helped me come up with some way to..."

Tom stopped in the middle of his sentence.

"Never mind."

Gene watched the expressions on his friend's face. Tom had turned his eyes toward the ceiling. He seemed to look away in a futile attempt to keep the tears from coming out of his eyes. He was quiet for a few minutes as he gathered his thoughts; then, he glanced at his friend.

"Gene, I need you to take over for me. I don't know how long I'll be gone, but I'll be gone as long as it takes to win her back. She wants to make a difference in Africa, and maybe I can prove to her I want to make a difference with her. I need to call Spencer and Brittany, but I don't know what to say."

"Don't worry about it. Leave it to Kathy and me. You go and be with your wife. You don't have to call the kids just yet."

Gene paused.

"I do have a question for you. You talked a lot about your dad. Have you resolved the issues you had with him?"

He saw Tom's jaw tighten. His eyes seemed to turn from

their blue to a steel gray as he narrowed his gaze to stare at Gene. Gene thought it must have been the light, but could it have been the anger piercing through from his soul?

"Just as I thought. You know God can help you with your anger. You have to do something that Lisa has had to do with you. You need to forgive him. Is he even still alive?"

"I don't know. I haven't seen or heard from him since I was…" Tom stopped again. Tom seemed to become more enraged at the thought. He balled his hands into fists. His countenance change as he held his lips tightly together and his face flushed.

"Your rage will not hurt your father, but it has hurt you and Lisa. I'm surprised you've kept it in as long as you have, but it's started to come out. It needs to be dealt with. If you keep this up, it will continue to hurt the two of you and others as well."

"I hate the man and what he did to all of us."

"You have to release the anger, Tom. It's the only way."

Tom leaned back in his chair. He swiveled in it until Gene could only see his profile. Then, Tom ran his fingers through his hair. He gripped his head as though his thoughts were tearing him apart.

"I know we are taught that men don't cry, but Tom, you have a ton of emotions that have to come out some way. You can either punch a wall and put a hole it in and possibly break your hand in the process or you can cry. And you know we are friends even though you are technically my boss."

Tom nodded without saying a word. He stared into the distance for a few moments.

"I don't know how," he said with a blank stare.

Gene moved closer to Tom and put one hand on his shoulder. He began to pray in a soft voice.

"Father, I lift up my friend, Tom, to You. Help him forgive his father. Help him to realize how much You love him."

As Gene prayed, Tom began to let down his emotional walls. Although Tom had told Christine a little about his childhood, he had kept many details to himself. He did discover there was something freeing about telling her what he'd gone through. He spent the next hour spilling his secrets out into the open. Through most of the conversation, Tom spoke almost in monotone; however, his emotions came to the surface when he talked about the last night he saw his father.

"I was 9 on the night my father was taken away in handcuffs, and my mother was taken away in an ambulance," Tom was trying to hold back his tears as he spoke. "I had gone to bed, but I woke up to the sound of him beating her. I snuck out of the house and got the neighbors to call the police. I remember my mother's face bruised and bloodied. She couldn't defend him this time. They'd been called so many times before. She was in the hospital for a couple of months, but she was never the same. Her eyes were haunted with the memories. She never spoke of my father again. She never talked about that night. When I saw Courtney's face, all of these memories started flooding back to me with a vengeance. Not just that night, but countless other nights. He'd beat me, and she'd come between us to take the beating. I couldn't sleep without seeing these pictures in my mind. I started drinking so I wouldn't see them. Not only did my mother never talk about my father to me again, she never allowed me to talk about him or what he'd done to either of us. It was as though he didn't exist. I had to keep it all inside. It made me so ashamed of myself. When my mother died, I thought the secrets died with her. I made do. I survived. I ignored the thoughts. I thought I'd beaten them."

Gene listened.

"Tom, you also need to get your anger out towards God."

Tom faced Gene.

"What do you mean?"

"You are angry because you feel God should have done something about your father and how he treated you and your mother, and you think He never did."

Tom looked confused.

"How did you know that?"

"It's only natural. If you have to yell, then do it. Admit it and then forgive God."

"I've never heard anything quite like that before," Tom stopped and digested what Gene said. "You are right though. I have been angry with God for not doing something about my father."

"Then, let it all out. Don't worry if you cry. You need to. I'm not going to judge you."

Tom nodded.

Tom stood up and started to pace the floor. He gripped his hands into fists. He wanted to punch the wall or a punching bag. Finally, he fell to his knees. He didn't hold back the tears, and he began to pound his fists on the hardwood floor.

"I hate you – Marvin Kinsey – for what you did to my mother and me," Tom screamed. "I hate you. I hate you."

He began to cry harder. Gene felt at a loss and sat in silence, praying under his breath as Tom spilled out his years of pent-up emotion. It was hard for Gene to watch this man who was usually so composed exhibit such raw emotion. He couldn't ever remember Tom raising his voice.

After several minutes, Tom stopped crying and yelling in anger. He sat on the floor and covered his face with his hands.

Gene put one hand on his shoulder.

"Now, forgive him and God. Come out of your prison," he said.

Tom kept his face covered for several minutes. Forgiving his father and God seemed like such a hard thing to do. He hated crying. His father had always made fun of him when he cried. He called Tom a sissy. He said real men didn't ever cry. Then, he said even more hurtful things. Even more memories Tom had suppressed over the years came flooding back. The anguish and torment spilled out through what seemed to Tom to be a bucket of tears.

Gene continued to pray for his friend as he released the torrent of emotions.

After several minutes of gut-wrenching emotion, Tom

became quiet. In a weak whisper, he said "I forgive you Marvin Kinsey, and I forgive you, God."

Tom remembered the last time he'd prayed with Gene. He felt different. This time, he felt he'd let go of something he'd carried for years. A tremendous weight had been rolled away. He wasn't suffocating any longer.

"How are you now?"

"Exhausted, but I feel like I'm 15 years younger," he said still seated on the floor.

"Now, you are ready to go see Lisa."

Tom nodded. He looked at his friend for a moment as if he was carefully choosing the right words to say.

"Gene, I'm making you a partner."

Gene was shocked. Tom had never said anything about a partnership.

"You've just gone through an emotional shock to your system. Now is not a good time to make rash decisions."

"This isn't a rash decision. I've been thinking about it for a while now. We'll work out the details. I've worked long and hard to make a company, but I've sacrificed everything to do it. I'm not doing it any more. This whole thing has made me realize how precious life is and how I've wasted so much time. And you have always been there. I have always been able to count on you. You've gone above and beyond. I need help, and you are the man to help me."

Tom sprung from his place on the floor and returned to his desk.

"You said Lisa has met a pastor?" Gene asked.

"Yes, there's a church involved with this project."

"What happened here today was great, but you probably should talk to someone else – someone professional. Her pastor friend might be able to help you."

Tom appeared not to be listening as a new flight to Nairobi leaving the next afternoon appeared on the screen. He pulled out a credit card and booked it on the spot.

Gene didn't say anything else until Tom turned his attention to him.

"Gene, I'm sure you are right, and about two days from now, I can ask him face-to-face. I'm going to need a ride to the airport."

Gene smiled.

"Yes, sir. Gene's taxi at your service."

Tom grinned and stuck out his hand. Gene grabbed his hand to shake it, but then, he pulled his friend close for a brief hug. Tom seemed surprised at the action.

"When does your flight leave?" Gene asked.

"2 p.m. tomorrow."

"I'll see you tomorrow then. You need to pack."

Tom smiled.

"Yes, I do."

Tom went to his bedroom and threw two suitcases onto the bed. He wasn't sure he would need them both. Most of his wardrobe consisted of business attire. He wasn't going to need that in Africa. Jeans and T-shirts? He had a few of those. That's what he needed to take. He needed work clothes. He had a feeling he had a job to do.

He gathered the photographs and Lisa's clues together and flipped through them once more. It would be about 7 p.m. Kenya time the day after his departure that Tom would reach Lisa. He wanted to relive those moments until he met her. He wanted to keep the reminders near him as he had a few hours in London before the next leg of his journey. He didn't want anything in that city to distract him.

That night when Tom closed his eyes, he envisioned Lisa sleeping next to him. He felt a huge weight had been lifted and without the aid of his bottle of Scotch, he slept for the first time in months.

17

Lisa tried to picture a happy reunion in her mind. She imagined those movies of people running through a field with their arms outstretched and joining in a hug and the man would spin the woman around. She chuckled wondering where that thought came from. Not happening, she thought. Would they just stand and stare at each other? Maybe he'd be angry with her? Maybe he'd want her to return home right away? Maybe he wouldn't even show up at all?

Matt noticed Lisa seemed agitated. He could tell she had a clock ticking in her brain. She was trying to figure out how many days it would take for Tom to show up, and by her estimation, the countdown was getting close.

"I probably should not have told you Tom visited my secretary," said Matt, interrupting her thoughts, as he sat next to her at the breakfast table.

Lisa tried to laugh.

"Why do you say that?"

"You've got that excited but worried look. I've seen it before. You're hoping for something good to happen, but you aren't sure it will," he said.

A few tears trickled down Lisa's cheeks. She's been trying to hold back the emotion.

"I am so tired of crying. You have no idea," she said.

Matt placed his hand on her shoulder.

"Let me say a little prayer for you, okay?"

Lisa nodded.

"Lord, I lift up Lisa to You now, and I ask You to give her peace. You know she desires to reconcile with her husband. I ask You to help them work through their differences. I've seen marriages thrive even after infidelity, and they can if both people will commit to the relationship. Let her know You love her today. In Jesus' name, I pray."

Matt patted her shoulder.

"We've got to get things rolling soon," he said with a smile and headed into the other room.

Lisa nodded and dried her eyes. She walked into her room to pack her camera batteries which she'd recharged overnight. It was going to be a long day of taking photos of construction.

It was a good thing Lisa had packed extra memory cards and an extra battery pack. She didn't know what she was going to do with all of the photos she had taken. She had far more than could ever be used in one lifetime much less one book. She snapped away without paying much attention to what she was doing. She tried to shut her mind and emotions down. It was a trick she'd learned over the years. She'd written a series of stories about soldiers returning from Iraq. During a 12-month span, she interviewed so many young men and women barely out of high school, who had lost limbs and been permanently scarred. It was a tough series. She'd cried so many nights while seeing their faces. Over time, she was able to shut out some of their pain; she knew then it was time to stop writing those stories. She'd turned off an emotional sensor in her brain, and she felt it made her less of a human being. She was less empathetic, and it showed in her work. She was so glad when that series was over. But today, she needed that mind trick. She needed to not feel. She prayed for healing or at least a temporary numbness of the pain and anxiety she felt. She just wanted it to go away. Could Tom's arrival heal that pain?

Lisa's sense of time disappeared as she worked, which was the whole idea behind the trip in the first place. She buried the nagging thoughts of Tom. It was an exhausting battle. On the drive back, she dozed off. When they arrived at the house, it was dark. Lisa was slow to move out of the van. She waited until everyone else had gotten off before she started to get out. She couldn't wait to climb into bed and sleep.

She heard Matt calling her name.

"Coming," she replied as she pulled out her camera gear. Her back had stiffened during the ride. She tried to stretch to make it feel a little better. She walked into the house with her head down as she made sure her camera bag was secured. She didn't see Matt and bumped into him.

"Sorry," she said.

As she raised her head, she noticed everyone from the team was in the room, and they were staring at her. She gave Matt a questioning gaze. He smiled and shook his head at her as she hear someone clear his throat.

"Angel," Tom said.

The camera bag slid off her shoulder and onto the floor. He walked toward her and pulled her close to him.

"I'm so sorry, Angel," he whispered into her ear. "I love you. I always have. Can you ever forgive me?"

Although stunned, she wrapped her arms tightly around Tom and closed her eyes. She heard several people in the room applaud. Then, the team members went to their respective rooms.

"Yes," she said. "I have forgiven you, and I'm sorry for the test I put you through."

Tom slowly moved back. He touched her cheek with his fingertips. Then, he turned on his charm and smiled at her.

"Did I pass?" he asked.

Lisa nodded as tears fell down her cheeks.

"One second," he said and walked toward the table.

She hadn't noticed a huge bouquet of roses.

"They're beautiful," she said.

He grabbed her hand, glancing at her palm where she'd cut herself after picking up the glass shards from the vase she'd smashed against the wall not long ago. He raised his eyebrow.

"I promise to try to never do anything else that will cause you to ruin a great vase," he said and flashed his smile. She'd missed that smile.

She felt her skin flush.

"It's okay. I deserved this not you," he said tracing his finger along the scar. "I was wrong."

She heard Matt clear his throat. She glanced behind her. Matt waved and grinned.

"Hi," he said.

"Tom, have you met Matt?" she asked.

"Briefly. Just before you came in."

"I'm going to bed, but before I do, I want you to know I'm here for both of you. Not now because I'm tired," Matt laughed.

Tom stuck out his hand to shake Matt's.

"I had a very good friend tell me I needed to talk to someone besides my wife; he said you might be the man," said Tom.

"In the few weeks I've known Lisa, I've found her to be a compassionate and caring person. I can make time to talk with you while I'm here, and my calendar will be open for you individually or the two of you together," he said. "Now, I'll leave you two alone."

Matt saluted and walked away. There was an awkward silence for a few minutes. Thoughts rushed through both of their minds, but neither was sure what to say.

"He seems like a great guy," said Tom.

Lisa nodded.

"He's helped me a lot. He's helped me put things in a different perspective," she said. "And he's just plain nice. He's genuine in his caring for the people here and back home."

She directed her gaze back to Tom and stared into his eyes.

"He also wants to see us get back together. He means it when he says he will help," she said.

140

"And I meant it when I said I'd talk to him. I've never admitted I need any help, and that's been one of my biggest problems."

He paused for a moment. Then, he smiled once again.

"I have something for you."

Underneath the table was a large basket. Inside it was the ugly pink bear and all of the cards and photographs she'd given as clues. There were four wrapped packages as well. She sat down at the table and opened them. She was confused at first when she found gauze, tape and other items from a first aid kit beneath the festive wrap, but she soon understood.

"I know that I can't undo the damage, but I want to help heal it," he said.

"Tom, I'm the only woman who understands your sense of humor," she said. "I get this. I really do."

"You got me thinking about the first bouquet and the aspirin," he said. "I know gauze and these other items can never mend you emotionally, and I don't take this lightly. Everything is over with Christine. I will never see her again."

Lisa nodded.

"And one other thing, I'm making Gene my partner. I've neglected my beautiful wife for too long. We got a huge contract, and I'm going to let him handle some things from now on so I can make sure this doesn't ever happen again."

Lisa looked surprised. She'd suggested to him he needed help, but he had never listened to her. He always wanted to do everything himself.

"So, Mrs. Kinsey, will you take your wayward husband back?" he said leaning forward to lightly kiss her lips. Without thinking she slightly turned her head away so he kissed her cheek instead.

"I never wanted to let you go," she said.

She looked at him and tried to figure out why she avoided his kiss. It was what she wanted, wasn't it? He looked hurt, but he smiled at her.

"You and I have a lot of talk about, and you look very tired. You should get some sleep. We have a long day in front of us tomorrow from what I can tell," he said.

"Yes, it's been a really long day. I fell asleep in the van," she said.

She walked into her room. He followed, but he stopped at the door.

"Good night, Angel," he said as he turned to walk down the hall.

"Where are you going?"

"I'm staying in Matt's room."

Lisa couldn't hide her shocked expression.

"You are staying with Matt?" she repeated slowly. "He already has a roommate."

"I asked him before you came in. There's another room for Jackson. That little move of yours confirmed it was the right thing for me to do."

"I'm sorry."

"I have my work cut out for me to repair the damage I've done. I won't force myself on you."

"You wouldn't be."

"Shakespeare had a line about that one too. Something about a woman protesting too much. I know I hurt you, but I'm going to do my best to show you I hate myself for what I did. It was more than just getting involved with Christine. I shut you out, and I've never done that before. You are important to me, Lisa. I can't live without you."

"I'm sorry."

"Don't be. I understand, and I expected you to act that way. We will work this out."

He reached out and pulled her close to him. She started to cry harder as he gently rocked her. She missed his embrace and how he'd hold her at night until she fell asleep. It felt so good to have his strong arms wrapped around her. More than anything this was what she wanted. She knew she could put the past behind them.

"I want all the emotional walls to come down," he whispered.

He stood there holding her until she stopped crying.

"I'll see you in the morning," he said and kissed the top of her forehead.

18

The wake-up call was always too early for Lisa. She'd never been a morning person anyway. She still hadn't completely adjusted to the time difference, and they spent long days in the villages either drilling or working on new construction about an hour away. And for most of the trip, she's lie in bed with her mind going a million different ways only to fall asleep right when it was time to wake up. On this morning, she was surprised to find Tom waking her. Tom functioned on very little sleep. She was never sure how he did it. All of their marriage, he was up well before dawn and stayed up late.

"Come on, Angel, we have work to do," he said as he kissed her on her forehead. She struggled to open her eyes to see her husband fully dressed in jeans and a T-shirt. She didn't even think he had those items in his closet at home.

"What are you doing?" she asked.

"I'm going to help build something today, and you, my beautiful one, are going to take photos."

Lisa was stunned.

"You are going out there today to build?" she repeated his words because she wasn't sure she'd heard him.

"Do you have a problem with that?"

"No just surprised."

He sat down on the bed next to her.

"I've been struggling with a lot of things like you have. I

144

want my life to make a difference too, and I want to be a part of your world again. Our world has changed, and we can't go back to what it was. I'm willing to change with it."

Lisa smiled.

"As much as I'd love to stay here with you, we have an orphanage to build. Now, get dressed before the van leaves you here," he said.

Lisa dressed and headed toward the van. She was still confused as Tom took her camera equipment from her. The orphanage wasn't as far from the house as the villages were. It needed to be closer to the city. Tom jumped in with both feet. He wasn't afraid to get dirty. They were still working on the building's framework, and he spent most of the day nailing boards.

Lisa watched him through her camera lens. He seemed to be getting along well with other members of the mission's team. They accepted him into the group no questions asked. They probably enjoyed having another set of hands to help them. He and Matt also worked in close proximity. She knew Matt wanted to get to know him better. Pulling down Tom's walls would take time, but Tom and Matt were a lot alike. They both had extroverted personalities and were charismatic.

Matt took a water break and walked over to chat with Lisa.

"Not quite what you expected?" he asked.

"I guess you could say that. I was surprised at how I reacted when he tried to kiss me. I guess he told you that."

"Yes, and even though this is an unorthodox counseling session I've done, it's all confidential. He expected you to react the way you did. He understands. As a matter of fact, he was afraid of what you'd do. You did better than he thought."

"What did he think I was going to do to him? Hit him?" she asked.

"Well, don't tell me the thought hadn't crossed your mind at some point."

"I threw a vase and cut open my hand. That's enough

violence for me."

She paused for a minute.

"I thought I'd forgiven him," she said as tears began to fall again. Lisa let out a disgusted groan. "I'm so sick of crying. When will I stop crying?"

"Crying is good, and sometimes, forgiveness takes time; healing takes time. Healing a broken heart is tricky, and Tom knows it. He's got some healing to do as well. But you've got a few things on your side. You have God, and you have a man who wants to work this out. He's not a man who's remorseful for getting his hand stuck in the proverbial cookie jar, but one who realizes he made a huge mistake. And I believe he's truly sorry."

Lisa nodded.

"And you have me," Matt grinned his California surfer smile. "I want to help you both through this."

Lisa laughed.

"I don't even go to your church."

Matt looked at her.

"The church isn't just a building. The church is people, and my job is to help hurting people."

"What about you? Who helps you? Who heals the wounds of someone who's lost his wife and is afraid to love again?"

Matt stared at her for a moment.

"I'm sorry. That just slipped out."

"I never thought of it that way. Are you sure you are supposed to be a writer, lady reporter? I think there might be some other gifts inside of you."

He smiled at her look of bewilderment.

"Compassion and empathy are huge when it comes to ministry. You can't be an effective missionary without them. You also have a lot of insight into people, and you may be right about me."

"Okay," she said.

"We'll chat again later," he said and made his way back to take up his drill.

Lisa stared at Tom. She still had images of him and Christine in her mind. She wished she could erase them. It wasn't going to be easy. She wondered what Matt meant by Tom having wounds that needed healing. As she watched him hammering some boards, he looked up and met her gaze. He smiled, and she felt embarrassed that he'd caught her staring. She tried to cover it up by raising her camera and turning the lens away from him.

While she focused her lens elsewhere, she heard footsteps and felt him getting close to her. He had decided to take a water break too. He stood close to her and leaned to whisper in her ear. She could feel his breath upon her face.

"I love you, Angel. You are still the most beautiful woman in the world."

As he departed, he gently kissed her cheekbone and stroked her face without her ever taking the camera down.

What was that feeling? She felt her pulse racing, and she was slightly out of breath. Those feelings of excitement at his presence she had not felt in a long time. She remembered when they first started dating and were first married that he only had to look at her and smile, and she'd swoon. With one touch, he started to melt away her anger.

She turned her lens toward him, and as she did, he looked up at her. He didn't give her the charismatic smile he gave the world, but he gave her a smile only she'd seen. With her telephoto lens, she could adjust it to see straight into his deep baby blues. Her heart began to beat quicker. She knew that look. All of a sudden it wasn't Tom and Christine she was seeing in her mind. As she saw that look, she remembered the passion they'd experienced throughout their marriage. Now she really needed a distraction or a cold shower.

She turned her attention to the people gathered to watch some of the construction and tried to breathe normally. Since they were in a highly populated area near Nairobi, people would stop and talk. The group's interpreter told them about the project along with the well-drilling project in the outer areas. Lisa had been listening to the interpreter as much as she could. She was learning to pick up a few Swahili words here and there. She found it fascinating, and the people who lingered seemed to as well. Some were more interested in her documenting them than the project at hand.

The crowd reaction would make some great color for her book. It was important to put as many faces with the project as possible.

She watched Jackson, who wasn't Grayson Devereux's son, the would-be politician to her any longer. He was Jack, someone committed to the project. He blended into the group so well. He didn't have an air of privilege about him. She knew he genuinely wanted to help.

Keeping focused was difficult. Although she'd tried to turn her attention to Jackson and to the others, she was so intrigued by the fact that Tom would travel halfway across the globe and immediately start working. He built a deck on their house once so Lisa had seen him with a hammer. He seemed energized even though she knew he had to be exhausted. As she watched him, she realized something about him had changed. He wasn't the same stressed-out, emotional wreck as the last time she saw him, the day when he announced he was having an affair and needed time. He had lost some weight. He looked pale, but remarkably, there seemed to be a vitality she hadn't seen in years. He was laughing with the men he was working with. He was enjoying being with them. She wondered how he'd react in the villages where the poverty was so overwhelming.

When she looked at him, she could see the 20 year-old she fell in love with.

On the ride back to the house, Tom and Lisa sat next to each other. He put one arm around her and held her hand with the other. Every touch seemed to kick another brick out of the wall she'd built. Several times, he leaned over and whispered "I love you, Angel" into her ear. At one point in the journey back, she rested her head on his shoulder and fell asleep. She'd missed the safety of his arms.

When they arrived back at the house, there was time for a

quick dinner before heading to their respective rooms. It had been a long and backbreaking day for the men.

"Are you hanging in there?" Matt asked Tom.

"You're a slave driver, Matt," he said.

"You've been a great help to us. Every set of hands makes the job so much easier."

Tom nodded.

"Good night, Angel," he said as he kissed her on the forehead.

"Good night," she replied and went to her room alone again.

Back in the room Tom shared with Matt, they sat across from each other on their single beds. Tom seemed at ease with Matt. They stayed up for several hours. Matt had no problems asking questions point blank. He asked Tom why he'd gotten involved with Christine, and he told Matt the same things he told Gene. He told him about the car accident and the flashbacks. He told him about the drinking. It was easier this time.

"What do you want, Tom?" Matt asked.

"I want my Lisa back. I want my Angel," he said.

"Why?"

"She's the love of my life."

"Tom, she feels the same way. She's been processing all the pain. I think she's on the healing path, and I think the two of you can heal together. I do want to work with you on the issues of abuse you suffered. I know you said you haven't wanted anything to drink, but I want to monitor that too. Those issues might take you a little longer, but I think in the end you will be stronger for it."

Tom nodded.

"Now, since I'm a slave driver. Go to sleep so I can wake you up again in the morning."

"Yes, sir!"

In her room, Lisa held the ugly pink bear close to her and cried softly. She wanted her husband with her. She'd slept alone for far too long. She was ready to move on or at least part of her was.

The next two days were much of the same. They were so

busy, filled with long hours of hard work. It was the final day of work for this group. They'd have a day to enjoy Nairobi before taking a long flight home. Lisa still had another week before she was scheduled to go home. They'd only been on the site for a few hours when Matt broke into her thoughts as he walked up next to her.

"We are ahead of schedule here. Tom has been a tremendous help in the few days he's been here, but the three of us are leaving."

Lisa was puzzled.

"Why?"

"Why do you ask so many questions, lady reporter?" he asked and laughed. "No time like the present."

Lisa and Tom got in the van. He held her left hand as he sat next to her. She leaned against him. She didn't feel all of the anger she'd felt a few days before although she knew there was some there. She felt her heart begin to race again as she drew close to him.

When they arrived back at the house, Matt ushered them into the living room.

Lisa sat in chair, and Tom sat on the couch. Matt moved opposite of them.

"This is not exactly the best situation for marriage counseling, but it's what we have," Matt said.

He had the attention of them both.

"I've talked to both of you separately. You have a milestone soon, and I have to help clear the air before then. Okay, this is the part I hate. I don't like playing referee, and I hope I won't have to with you. I only have one question for you. Have you even talked to each other since the affair happened?"

Tom and Lisa glanced at each other. She looked down and remembered their strained phone conversations.

"Not really," said Tom. "Just on the phone."

"That's what I thought. You can't ignore this any longer. As you both have found out, ignoring emotions and burying them without dealing with them will have disastrous results. So today, the cycle ends."

Lisa and Tom nodded.

"First, we are praying. Heavenly Father, we ask You to come and heal this relationship, and these two people who want to restore and repair their lives," he said.

Matt took a deep breath.

"Let's lay some ground rules. No name calling; no yelling at each other. If you need to yell, don't direct it at your spouse. No throwing anything. I don't think we have any crystal vases, Lisa. Most importantly, choose your words carefully. Don't say anything you will regret as soon as it comes out of your mouth. There's no taking words back. Once they are out, you have to live with them forever."

Matt looked at both of them.

"Okay, you both get to say your piece. Lisa, you can go first."

Lisa thought for a minute.

"I don't have anything except to ask 'Why?' Why did you do this to me? Why did you do this to us? And with a woman who is young enough to be your daughter! And then, you ran away. Why did you leave me?"

"I'm not the only one who ran away," Tom shot back.

Matt whistled.

"Time out. Tom, it's not your turn. Let Lisa finish."

"I've been angry. Yes, I smashed your roses against the wall, and it felt really good when I did. And maybe I did run away. I have felt like I was dry, empty, useless. The kids left; the newspaper cut me out. Then you – you of all people. I never thought you'd leave me. You've always been there. Those days alone. I felt like I'd died. I didn't want to live. I felt I'd wasted 25 years."

Tears began to flow much to Lisa's frustration.

"I'm sick of crying," she let out aggravated yell. "I thought this was over. I haven't cried in two days."

She stood up and walked over to a window to compose herself. She leaned against a wall, hating herself for crying once again. Tom moved as though he was going to walk over to her.

Matt motioned for him to stop.

"Let her get this out," he said.

She took several deep breaths.

"And then, out of nowhere, I discover there was one who had never left me even though I'd walked away. He called me home, and He led me here."

She turned back to look at Tom.

"Since I arrived here, I've felt like I had a purpose again. I felt useful and needed. Most of all, I finally feel alive. And I want to be over all of these horrible feelings that still make me cry."

She walked back to her chair and sat down.

"I can't think of anything else," she said and shook her head. "I've cried, thrown vases, yelled. I hope there's nothing left. I hope it's all gone by now. I wanted to lash out at you, but I can't."

Matt allowed for a long pause before he turned to Tom.

"Now you can speak."

"Why? If you'd asked me that the day boarded the plane, I didn't have the answer, but all I've been doing is asking myself that question since," he said. "And now, I do know the answer. I never talked about my dad to you. I hated him. He drank; he beat my mother. I know there were other women. I didn't understand it at the time. One night, he came home, drunk like he always was. I woke up to hear my mother screaming and begging him to stop. I crawled out of my window and beat on the door until the neighbors called the police. I ran back into the house to find my mother covered in blood, and my father being arrested. They put her on a stretcher and took her away. When I saw Courtney in that accident, I immediately saw the flashback of my mom. I'd tried so hard to forget that night. I'd tried not to remember my mother's face. The police tried to shield me, but I saw her. I thought she was dead. It was an image that was burned on my brain forever. I'd ignored those feelings and memories for so long. I'd pushed them down and buried them deep."

Now, Lisa was crying for other reasons as she listened to him.

"I remember feeling like I'd failed my mother even though she lived through that night. I was supposed to protect her I thought.

Several months before Brittany went away to college, I felt like I lost you emotionally. You pulled away from me. I started to feel like you didn't need me. Brittany's senior year you were involved in so many projects in the community. You had so many things you were working on for the paper. And when your world started to fall apart, I had no idea how to reach you. I couldn't fix your problems. It was that sense of hopelessness and helplessness once more. That's not an emotion I know how to deal with. I fix things. I'm the strong one."

Tom was agitated. He needed to pace while he talked.

"You felt useless? Everything I'd done and worked for was to give you and our children a good life. I had done that up until now. You closed into your world. You pushed me away."

He stood still and took a deep breath.

"I felt alone. I started drinking more. I couldn't sleep. I kept seeing my mother's face and Courtney's face. It haunted me. I started staying at the office because I didn't want you to know I was drinking. And I was having a problem with it. It was getting worse. I have always been the strong one. I never needed anyone. My dad told me to never need anyone, always take care of yourself. Be a man; don't cry. Don't show weakness."

He turned to look at Matt.

"Then, Christine showed up to work on this project. And Christine wanted me from the very beginning. She wanted to be with me, not for anything I could do for her. She wanted me – Tom. At least I thought she did, but I think there were other things now that I look back on it. She listened to me. She connected with me. She seemed to understand. I felt both sides closing in. I pushed her away so many times. You aren't the only one who wants to make a difference in this world. I couldn't help you, and my kids didn't need me. The stress of this contract was too much."

Tom paused, wondering what details to leave in, what to say.

"This contract was high stakes. We were competing with several other companies. One night, Christine came back to the office. I had been drinking to ease the pain I felt. Every time, I closed my eyes...I drank so much because I wanted it to stop."

He looked at Lisa.

"I tried to leave, but I was in no condition to drive. I've never been that wasted in my life. I never wanted to lose control like my father did. Even in college, with all the clubs I was part of, I stayed away from all the drinking. But that night, I think I might have passed out. I don't remember anything else except I woke up the next morning when your text came through. She was gone. I locked myself in my office. I thought all day about what to say to you. I couldn't hide it. I didn't want to. Besides the blinding headache, I felt a huge sense of guilt and shame. I'd done something I never wanted to do. I thought about my mother, and how my father had cheated on her. Strike one against me was the drinking; strike two against me was Christine. What was strike three? You know I don't even know where my father is. They took him away that night. Without my mother to defend him, they finally took him away. She was unconscious. She couldn't sign a statement or tell the officers it was a misunderstanding."

Lisa stared at him.

"In London, Gene talked to me like no one had ever talked to me. He made me come face-to-face with me. He did exactly what I told you I needed to do when I walked out. I needed to find out what was wrong with me. He made me look deep inside at things I didn't want to look at. London was extremely uncomfortable for me for more reasons than one."

Tom moved closer to Lisa and sat down so he could look into her face.

"Then, Gene shared his faith. He shared his experiences with me, and I asked Gene to pray for me."

Tom smiled and shook his head.

"I have never experienced anything like that before. The weight of the world rolled off of me. I felt like a new person."

He paused. There was a joy on his face.

"I knew I had to come home to you, and things started

falling into place. I was able to wrap up the deal not long after. I saw Christine in a restaurant. I made it clear it was over."

He reached out for Lisa's hand.

"When I got home and you weren't there, the thought of losing you became more real. It scared me. I've never been so scared in my life. Gene and Kathy were there again for me. And Gene's final confrontation came right before I found a great flight here. He made me deal with my anger concerning my father. I pounded on our wooden floors and screamed. I forgave my father."

"I wish you had told me all of this sooner. I would have been here to help you," said Lisa.

"You are right, and you probably would have been there if I'd have said something. I didn't know what to say. I didn't know how to say it. Like I said, I've always been the strong one. That's what I was taught. Be the man. Be strong. Don't be weak. In trying to be strong, I found out just how weak I really was."

She needed to hear the things he'd said. Over the past couple of weeks, his actions had spoken volumes, but there were still things she needed to hear.

"It sounds to me that in the time the two of you have been apart you've done a lot of soul searching. You've reconnected with your faith, and you've both asked God for restoration in your marriage," said Matt. "You've also tried to get rid of some damaging emotions."

They both nodded. Tom stood up.

"There's something I have to do. I'll be right back."

"Lisa, are you okay?" Matt asked her as Tom left the room.

"Yes. I think so. All I know is that I don't want to cry anymore."

Tom came back quickly.

"Tom, before you do anything. I have to ask Lisa a question in front of you. Lisa, I know you said you've forgiven Tom, but I need you to look directly at him and tell him you forgive him. You also need to release any feelings of revenge you have. Tom's already told you that he's working to forgive his dad. In a way, it was that toxic unforgiveness that opened the door for the way he treated you. Tom became the thing he hated."

Tom sat down on the couch next to Lisa's chair. Lisa looked uncomfortable at first, but she turned to give him her full attention. She'd said those words so many times she wasn't sure she even believed them any longer. The feelings didn't change. Surely, there should be some kind of feeling to go along with them. She took a deep breath. She wanted to be able to feel like she had forgiven him with no anger popping up and no pain.

"I forgive you," she whispered. "I don't hold this against you, and I want to move ahead."

"I do, too," he said as he got on one knee in front of Lisa. He took her hand and removed her rings, and he pulled out a small velvet box from his pocket.

"I promised you 26 years ago when I gave you your first ring that I'd replace it one day. After these past few months, I couldn't think of a better time."

He opened the box and showed her a one-carat marquis-cut diamond with a band encrusted with smaller diamonds. Lisa sat stunned as Tom pulled the ring out of the box and slid it and her wedding band back onto her finger.

"Lisa Kinsey, will you marry me, again?" he asked and smiled.

She looked into his blue eyes and found herself getting lost. Those butterflies had grown.

"Yes, Tom Kinsey, I will," she smiled as she leaned forward to kiss him. "And this time, I promise not to get so involved with my world that I forget the most important person to me."

"I promise to do the same."

"Well, it looks like my work is done for today," said Matt. "You may need me again. If you do, you know how to reach me."

The couple looked at him, and Tom stood up.

"Lisa, how do you feel?"

"Like that journalism major who bumped heads with a good-looking business major," she said as she touched Tom on the cheek.

"I'm headed back to the jobsite."

"No, wait," said Tom. "Tomorrow is our 25th anniversary. Would you remarry us?"

"Now?"

"Yes," said Lisa. "What did you say to me earlier? 'Why do you ask so many questions?' and 'No time like the present?'"

"I don't know if I have that book or not. Let me see what I can find. Give me a minute. I may have to play it by ear."

He left the room, and Tom moved to his knees and slid close to Lisa.

"Can we put the past in the past and look forward to our future together?" he asked as he took both of her hands into his. "I can't undo any of it, but I want to move ahead."

He reached out with his right hand to touch her cheek. He leaned forward to kiss her lips. Lisa was relieved that her feelings of anger were gone, and she was able to return his kiss with a fire she hadn't felt in years.

"Okay, you two. Wait until after the wedding," Matt joked as he came back. "No book. I think I've done this enough, but I'll have to improvise. Let's move some furniture and make a little room."

Tom and Lisa obliged.

"Give each other your rings back for now. Turn and face each other."

Lisa and Tom gave him their bands, and Lisa put her diamonds on her right hand.

"Marriage isn't just a legal contract as the world sees. God sees it as a spiritual union. With Christ at the center of your marriage, you aren't promised a happily-ever-after in the sense that you will never encounter any problems, but if you place your faith and trust in Him, you will be able to weather any storm that comes your way."

Matt paused.

"Okay, this is the place where I'm going to depart a little. The two of you have tried to do this on your own, but you realized you can't do it alone. Let Him be at the center of your relationship this time."

He smiled, and Lisa and Tom both smiled and nodded.

"Back to what I remember from the script. I want you to repeat after me. I, Tom, what is your full name?"

"You want me to say 'I, Tom, what is your full name?'" Tom joked. "It's Thomas David."

"I, Thomas David, take you,"

"Elizabeth Grace," Lisa interrupted.

"I, Thomas David, take you Elizabeth Grace to be my lawfully wedded wife," Matt started.

"Do you mind if I take it from here?" Tom interrupted.

"Not at all."

"I, Thomas David, take you, Elizabeth Grace, to be my lawfully wedded wife. I'm thankful to have had you by my side for 25 years. I wouldn't trade them for anything in the world. I promise to love, honor and cherish you. Thank you for reminding me of the reasons why I wanted to marry you in the first place. And thank you for giving me a second chance. I will be there in sickness and health and in the good and bad. I promise to love and cherish you. I've loved you, but I haven't cherished the gift that you are. You are the only woman I want now and forever."

"Great adlib," Matt said.

"Theater training," Tom said with a wink and a smile.

"Elizabeth Grace, do you want to adlib too?"

Lisa smiled and nodded.

"Yes, I think I do. I, Elizabeth Grace, take you, Thomas David, as my lawfully wedded husband. I wouldn't have missed the last 27 years, I'm adding in the two years we dated, for anything. You are the man of my dreams. I promise not to look back on anything in our relationship except the good. I believe in second chances, and I believe we are doing this the right way. Several things brought me through this ordeal. One was a Bible verse that told me love never failed. There was a visit to the lake and a stranger came up to me to tell me it was going to be okay. There was this surfer-looking preacher who also gave me hope. And then, there was this sonnet by my favorite author, William Shakespeare, who wrote love was an ever-fixed mark that could look on tempests and not be shaken. I have to admit I was shaken for a little while, but even in that time, I still loved you. My love didn't shake even though my emotions did. I will love you forever, Thomas David. You have my heart."

"Let me see your wedding bands."

Matt placed them in the palm of his hand.

"These rings are circular, signifying a never-ending love the two of you share. Whenever you wear them, remember that love. Never forget the promises you've made to each other today."

Matt handed Tom Lisa's ring.

"Place it on her hand and repeat after me, 'Lisa, with this ring I thee wed.'"

"With this ring, I thee wed – again," he said obeying Matt's instructions.

Lisa followed, and Matt instructed Lisa to do the same with his ring.

"Since you are already married, I give you a blessing for a wonderful marriage for years to come. May you never lose sight of your love for one another, and may you always remember how much God loves you and wants to help you in your daily lives. Tom, you may kiss your bride."

Tom placed one hand on either side of Lisa's face. He gently pulled her close to him and softly kissed her lips. He could still taste some of her salty tears.

"I love you," he said.

She remembered their wedding kiss. This kiss brought back a rush of emotions like she'd felt on that day – so young and ready to conquer the world with just him and love.

He moved his hands down her body to her waist as he began to passionately kiss her.

"Okay. I'm gone," said Matt.

Lisa laughed. Tom released her, and she gave Matt a tight hug.

"Thank you, Matt. Thank you for everything."

"Happy anniversary, lady," he replied.

Matt tried to shake hands with Tom, but Tom gave him a short hug.

"Thank you, my new friend. Talking with you these past several nights has really helped me put things in perspective."

"We aren't done, but it can wait. There are some things that are more important," said Matt.

Tom wrapped his arm around his wife's waist and drew her close. She nuzzled into his neck and kissed him.

"You're welcome. I couldn't be any happier for you. I guess that means I've lost a roommate?" he said and laughed.

"Definitely. No more roommate for Matt," she said without removing her eyes from her husband's face.

Tom glanced at her.

"Really Mrs. Kinsey?" Tom raised one eyebrow.

Lisa smiled at him a smile he knew well.

"Well, it wouldn't be appropriate on our wedding night, now would it?"

"Yup. That's my cue. I'm outta here," Matt said as he headed out the door.

"I know that I still have a lot to work on, and I'm asking for your help to make it through," Tom said to Lisa.

"I will be there for you," she said and kissed him.

"I'm counting on it."

"I don't have an anniversary present for you."

"You are all I need, Mrs. Kinsey," Tom replied.

"Promise?"

"I promise," he said as he swung her up into his arms to carry her across the threshold to her room.

Epilogue

Lisa's formal dining room table was dressed with her finest linen tablecloths and adorned with her wedding china. Every detail was perfect from the beautiful turkey to the crystal glasses to her best silver flatware. Along with the turkey, there was a ham, dressing, sweet potatoes and green bean casserole. Tom stood at the head of the dining room table and tapped his crystal glass with a knife.

"Could I get everyone's attention?" asked Tom.

The guests quieted and turned toward their host.

"Last Thanksgiving, I wouldn't have imagined what a difference a year could make. It was one of the darkest days of my life," said Tom. "I'd returned home from London to find an empty house. The person who meant the most to me wasn't here, and I didn't know where she was. That was my own fault."

He motioned at Lisa to come and stand beside him. He paused as she took her place next to him, and he kissed her and whispered that he loved her.

"There are so many things I'm thankful for," he continued.

"To Gene and Kathy, you have always been great friends, but Gene, you will never know how much you've changed my life through the tough words you spoke to me a year ago. I needed to hear those things even though I didn't want to. You've caused my business to flourish, and you've taken it to a level I never dreamed possible. Promoting you was one of the best business decisions I've ever made."

Gene and Kathy were seated next to each other. They smiled as Gene grabbed Kathy's hand and squeezed it.

"Matt, you will never know how much we appreciate everything you've done. I think you were probably still in middle school when Lisa and I first got married, but it would have saved us so much heartache if we'd known someone like you then. You have become a great friend, and you've inspired me. You've taught me so much in this past year. I feel like you are the brother I never had. I appreciate you taking your time away from your family to be here."

"There's pumpkin pie there later," Matt said.

"Brittany and Spencer, we love you and are thankful for you. We're sorry for keeping you in the dark and for not having a proper Christmas celebration last year. I know we didn't get home from Africa until Dec. 23, but who doesn't love shopping at midnight right before Christmas?"

Brittany shook her head and looked at Kathy's teenage daughter.

"I'm not doing that this year," she said.

"No, we will be here, and the tree is going up this afternoon," said Lisa.

"I'm also thankful for my lovely bride. I had forgotten how much I loved the one person I promised to love all of my life, and she gave me a wake-up call I'll never forget. Lisa, you will always be the love of my life, and I'm thankful I can still call you my wife after what we've been through."

He leaned over and kissed her.

"Okay lovebirds, enough," Matt said and laughed. "No, seriously. When I grow up, I want to be just like you."

"Thanks Matt."

"Now for some news. Lisa's book is finished, and it's being marketed and sold through the newspaper. Lisa and I are entering a new phase of our lives. Working in Africa was an incredible experience for both of us. As you probably also know, now that Mr. Devereux's money has been sunk into the Africa mission, Jack has decided not to run for any office, at least not for now. The Senate can wait. He and his wife, Jamie, overseeing the foundation his father started, and he's going to be doing humanitarian projects in not only Africa, but in other third world nations too. During our time in Africa this year working closely with him before and after Christmas, Jack has asked Lisa and me to work with him. Matt will also be part of this equation."

Tom noticed a few surprised faces. He nodded in Matt's direction.

"I'm resigning from my church as pastor. I'm going to be moving to Africa soon. I'm going to miss it here, but my heart pounds when I'm helping the people over there. That's where I want to be," said Matt.

Tom continued.

"There's still a lot of work to be done. Lisa and I will be heading back in January so we want to make the most of this time all of us are together. While I will still be the controlling partner in the business, Gene is taking over the daily operations. We are thankful for each one of you here today. Last, but definitely not least, we are grateful to God for giving us a second chance with each other and with life. We believe this is just the beginning."

After the Thanksgiving banquet, Matt and Kathy helped Lisa clear the table and wash dishes as Tom, Brittany and Spencer began to pull out the Christmas decorations.

"You know, I was skeptical when you first stepped into my office on the verge of tears when I asked about your husband," said Matt.

"I was too."

"I've married a lot of couples in my short time in the ministry, and you seem happier and more in love than many of the ones standing at the altar."

"I went to Africa with a small hope that I'd see my husband again. I didn't tell you at the time, but I feared a divorce decree showing up in Africa or going home to find the locks changed and all my worldly goods at the thrift shop. Tom surprised me, and every day, he lets me know he loves me. So yes, Matt, I am the happiest woman in the world. Even after our vow renewal, there have been challenges, but I know that together with God, Tom and I can get through anything. He's a brand new man, and I've changed as well. And we have you to thank for so much, such as getting Tom the counseling he needed so he hasn't had a drink in a year now."

Tom walked into the kitchen to see them chatting.

"Mind if I interrupt?"

"Not at all, Tom. I was just telling your wife that she looks like a woman in love," Matt said.

Tom took her in his arms and smiled at her.

"Matt, I think you are right, and as long as I live, I will try to keep her looking that way."

Follow Charmain Z. Brackett on Facebook at
www.facebook.com/thekeyofelyon or @CZBrackett on Twitter.
Visit her website at www.charmainzbrackett.com